GLIMMER TRAIN STORIES

EDITORS
Susan Burmeister
Linda Davies

ASSISTANT EDITOR
Scott Allie

EDITORIAL ASSISTANT
Florence McMullen

CONSULTING EDITOR
Anne M. Callan

COPY EDITOR
Mark Morris

COMPUTER WIZARD
Michael Brown

COVER ILLUSTRATION
Jane Zwinger

STORY ILLUSTRATIONS
Jon Leon

LAST PAGE ILLUSTRATION
Bernard Mulligan, Rep. of Ireland

TYPOGRAPHY/LAYOUT
Paul O. Giesey/Adcrafters

PUBLISHED QUARTERLY
in February, May, August, and November by
Glimmer Train Press, Inc.
812 SW Washington Street, Suite 1205
Portland, Oregon 97205-3216 U.S.A.
Telephone: 503/221-0836
Facsimile: 503/221-0837

Glimmer Train (ISSN #1055-7520) is published quarterly, $29 per year in the U.S., by Glimmer Train Press, Inc., Suite 1205, 812 SW Washington, Portland OR 97205. Second-class postage paid at Portland, OR, and additional mailing offices. POSTMASTER: Send address changes to Glimmer Train Press, Inc., Suite 1205, 812 SW Washington, Portland, OR 97205.

ISSN # 1055-7520, ISBN # 1-880966-04-2, CPDA BIPAD # 79021

BOOKSTORES: *Glimmer Train Stories* is available through these distributors:
Bernhard DeBoer, Inc., 113 E. Centre St., Nutley, NJ 07110
Bookpeople, 7900 Edgewater Dr., Oakland, CA 94621
Ingram Periodicals, 1226 Heil Quaker Blvd., LaVergne, TN 37086
IPD, 674 Via de la Valle, #204, Solana Beach, CA 92075
Pacific Pipeline, 8030 S. 228th St., Kent, WA 98032
Ubiquity, 607 Degraw St., Brooklyn, NY 11217

Printed on recycled, acid-free paper.

Subscription rates: One year, $29 within the U.S. (Visa/MC/check). Air mail to Canada, $39; outside North America, $49. Payable by Visa/MC or check for U.S. dollars drawn on a U.S. bank.

Attention short-story writers: We pay $300 for first publication and one-time anthology rights. Please include a self-addressed, sufficiently stamped envelope with your submission. **Manuscripts accepted in January, April, July, and October.** *Send a SASE for guidelines.*

*D*edication

Winter sets in
and there are people squatting outside,
rocking back and forth on their heels
trying to warm themselves,
faces burning from the cold.

We dedicate this issue to those of you
who make the world
a little warmer,
a little safer,
a little less hungry,
a little less lonely,
on these cold days
and nights.

See you in spring.

Susan Burmeister   Linda Davis

CONTENTS

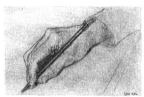

CONTENTS

Gary D. Wilson

This is the sole remaining photographic record of my existence before the flood that destroyed virtually all of my family's possessions (when I was seven). I'm about three years old in the picture, but I have so little recollection of my life from that time, I have no idea where the picture was taken or on what occasion. It's possible that this is not me at all, but my brother, who bears a striking resemblance to me.

Gary D. Wilson, who is married and has two sons, writes and teaches fiction workshops for Johns Hopkins University in Baltimore. He was born and reared in Kansas, and earned an M.F.A. from Bowling Green State University, Ohio, where he studied under Philip F. O'Connor. He has taught at various colleges and universities in the U.S., and spent two years teaching high school English for the Peace Corps in Swaziland, Africa. Wilson's fiction has appeared in numerous publications, including *The William and Mary Review*, *Witness*, *Kansas Quarterly*, *Wisconsin Review*, *Nimrod*, *Sun Dog*, *Amelia*, *City Paper* of Baltimore, *Outerbridge*, *Descant*, *Quartet*, *Green's Magazine*, *Cottonwood Review*, and *Itinerary* (now *Mid-American Review*).

GARY D. WILSON
What Happens Instead

We're at breakfast. My wife has already left for work. An early meeting, and she won't be home again until late. Which leaves me with Louie, our five-year-old son, and John, our eight-year-old. Louie sits at one end of the table, John opposite me. Mornings have never been our best time together.

We've just finished eating—grapefruit, toast, cereal. John asks for another grapefruit. A reasonable request, but I say no. Not that we don't have more—there's a whole boxful. It's the effort. The tedium of cutting it section by section so juice won't squirt everywhere. So I say no, he can have an orange. I tell him it's an orange or nothing.

He gets an orange. But before he peels it, he drinks the rest of his grapefruit juice from the bowl. There's a seed. He spits it on the table. I tell him to pick it up. He picks it up and shoots it at his brother. I tell him to put it in the bowl. He turns the bowl over on the table. His brother giggles.

"Settle down, John," I say.

He makes a face.

"I said settle down."

"Nanny-nanny-poo-poo."

"John—"

"Stick your head in doo-doo."

"All right. Go to your room."

"What'd I do?" he whines.

"Just go."

"It's Louie's fault. He made me do it."

"Now!"

"Not unless he goes too."

"I'm counting to three, John. One. Two. Three."

He doesn't move.

I stand up. "You'd better get moving."

"You can't make me."

"What?"

"You can't make me."

"Goddamnit, when I say something—"

I raise my hand. He flinches.

I flinch.

Thanksgiving. I'm twelve. Everybody's there—aunts, uncles, grandparents, cousins—all around the table, all set for a great feast. The best ever, they're saying, when he begins glaring at me and tells me not to eat some way or another and I answer him with a dirty look and that's why he hits me, he says later, that's why he stands and swings the full width of the table, backhanding me with a blow that knocks me off my chair and into the wall several feet behind me. I lie there, holding my head, the rich rusty taste of blood in my mouth. He's waiting for me to cry. He wants to see tears of remorse, guilt over having forced him to do what he's done. To hell with him. He turns and stomps off to another room. And now, as if all that isn't enough, my mother rises to tell me in front of God and everybody that I should be ashamed, that the whole thing is my fault and my father will be so upset he won't be able to finish his dinner. I can either apologize immediately or go to my room until I do, no matter how long it takes. But I have no intention of apologizing. Ever. The old bastard can starve as far as I'm concerned.

I lower my hand.

"I hate you, I hate you, I hate you, I hate you!" down the hall to his room, door slamming.

If it could only end there. John going off throwing a fit and coming back ten minutes later, smiling, telling me a joke the way kids do. We'd have a good laugh, a couple of hugs, then set off for school one big happy family again.

But nothing's that easily framed. It spills over the edges. Loses definition. Makes a mess.

What happens instead is this.

He comes out of his room, backpack in hand, the anger gone, but the hurt remaining in his eyes.

"Let's go," he says.

For the first time I can remember there is no fight over who sits where in the car. Louie jumps in back, John in front. Traffic isn't even as bad as it can be. The lights favor us. We manage a couple of halfhearted smiles at each other. I pat John's leg, reach back to squeeze Louie's hand.

"Knock-knock," I say.

Louie loves knock-knock jokes. "Who's there?"

"Amos."

"Amos who?"

"A mosquito just bit me on the knee."

Louie laughs.

John says to stop.

At school I find a safe place next to the curb to let John out. I put my arm around him and give him a hug. I say, "I know I'm not supposed to do this right here in front of everybody, but I'm going to anyway." And I kiss him.

He gets out. I say, "Have a nice day. I'll see you after school. Mama put a nice surprise in your lunch. I think you're going to like it."

He walks up the walk into the crowd.

Then I take Louie on to his school. A quiet trip. He sucks his thumb most of the way, which he usually does when he's worried about something. In this case, me. Whether because I got mad I'm going to leave him and his brother and mother. That's what he worries about most.

When we get to his classroom, I help him put things into his cubby. "Bye-bye," he says. I hug him good-bye. He starts playing and I stop to ask his teacher a question before I go. He sticks his head out of the tent house. I wave. He comes over and hugs my leg. "Bye-bye," he says. "See you after school," I say.

I leave. The door opens behind me. "Bye-bye, Papa," he says, "bye-bye." I wink until the crack in the door closes.

I barely make it up the steps to my door. There're thirty-eight in all and each one seems more tiring than the last. Then, standing there looking into that dark house, it's all I can do to put the key into the lock. It's like going back to a place where someone you loved has died.

I try working. I sit at my desk, get everything out. I pop my knuckles, stretch my neck, adjust my chair. And I stare.

I go to the kitchen for coffee, let the cat in, feed him, let him out, top off my cup. Still nothing.

I pick up pajamas, go to the bathroom, call my wife. She's sympathetic but says she's awfully busy and we'll have a long talk about it after she gets home.

I tell myself I'm being ridiculous. That even if I can't work, I can at least do something useful.

So I phone in catalogue orders. Perfect, I think. Repetitive and painless. Fill out forms and make calls. Converse with disembodied voices. Efficient, dispassionate, to the point.

"Wagoner's. Please give your name as it appears on the mailing label of your catalogue."

My name.

"Your address?"

My address.

"In the upper right-hand corner of the label is a number following the word *Code*. Would you read that, please?"

The number.

"The first item you wish to order, beginning with the item number."

Item and number. *I nearly hit my kid today.*

"Quantity?"

Quantity. *Hard. I mean really whacked him. Almost.*

"Color?"

Color. *Does that make me a bad person? Because I got that mad?*

"Size?"

Size. *Of course it doesn't, does it?*

"Price?"

Price. *I'm just feeling guilty is all. Right?*

"Do you wish to have the item gift wrapped?"

And so on. Which takes me until noon, when I decide to eat because that's what you're supposed to do then. I have one of my favorite meals: cold fried chicken breast, sliced green peppers, and buttered bread. But nothing tastes quite right. The peppers are end-of-season strong, the bread is stale, the chicken too greasy. I dump it and read the funnies from yesterday's paper, but there doesn't seem to be anything to laugh at, and I begin thinking about what my sons are thinking while they're eating. John hating me and loving his mother when he takes the grapefruit she fixed out of his lunch box. Louie peering hopefully over his food at the door I left by, his heart sinking every time it opens and it isn't me he sees. Or maybe they've forgotten the whole thing, filed it away, so to speak, until twenty years from now when they try to dredge it up for their analysts as an example of why it's been so hard for them to form meaningful relationships in their lives. If I were rich and famous, they could write a book about me and I could make it up to them that way. They could go on talk shows, John voicing righteous indignation over how their lives have been ruined, Louie casting soulful, wounded glances toward his brother at appropriate times. They'd make a good team. If they worked at it, they could promote a whole new theory: that the propensity for outbursts of uncontrollable anger is as genetically determined as hair or eye color or early onset of heart disease. Examples would be their own father (me), their grandfather (who, they've heard, was a man with a quick and awesome temper), and last but not least their great-grandfather (who, according to legend, once tore a car apart with his bare hands and knocked out a particularly irksome bull with one swing of his fist). The clincher, of course, would be that they see the same traits in themselves and that that's the reason they've never married or had children. All manner of offers for comfort and support would then roll in. Mainly money, since people are more prone to give it than true sympathy. With the funds they could establish the Caulkins Institute for the Study of Father/Son Relationships, a well-respected and well-endowed think tank engaged in the psychological alchemy of transmuting misery into happiness. It would be at once a self-limiting and self-perpetuating enterprise. They'd be set up for life, with me to thank for it.

Nanny-nanny-poo-poo, stick your head in doo-doo.

I go for a walk. I read a book. Three o'clock comes quickly.

"You know what?" Louie asks as soon as I pick him up.

"What?"

"My teacher said—"

"Miss Johnson?"

"Sure Miss Johnson, who do you think?"

"Might have been Mr. Lamarsky."

He finds me in the rearview mirror, shakes his head, looks away.

"You gonna talk to me?" I say.

"Maybe."

"Or are you gonna punish me?"

"Maybe." A quick smile.

"So what'd she say?"

"Who?"

"Miss Johnson."

"She said I didn't have to worry."

"About what? Is something wrong?"

"She said even if you were gone, you'd still be here."

"Oh yeah?"

"She said nothing ever really goes away. It's still there, even if you can't see it. Is that true?"

"I don't know."

"Is it like ghosts and stuff?"

"I doubt it."

"Are ghosts real, Papa?"

"No," I say, perhaps too quickly, too forcefully.

"Can they walk through walls and doors and everything?"

"No."

"Then how do they do it?"

I don't answer and he seems content to leave the question hanging as he sucks his thumb and watches for cars with pop-out lights the rest of the way to John's school.

I park behind the building as I always do. I go in the door, down the hall toward the cafeteria where his after-school group meets, and through a second door. I see him before he sees me. He's playing a board game. He's animated, smiling, apparently having a good time. He looks up. I wave. He must have been expecting someone else.

We're eating dinner together, the boys and I. Normally we don't. Normally my wife and I eat later, using the time to catch up with one another on the day's events. But she called and said she was running so far behind at work she was going to have to stay to get at least some of it finished. She was sorry. She knew it had been a rough day for me, too, and we could still have that talk when she got home, if I wanted to. Hugs and kisses to the boys, since she doubted she'd see them before bedtime.

We're having macaroni and cheese and carrot sticks. My sons love it. I can hardly force it down.

"Are there seconds?" Louie asks.

"Enough for a small helping each," I say.

"But I'll still be hungry," he says.

"Take this then." I hand him my bowl.

"Why does he get all of it?" John says. "He's already had more than anybody else."

"No he hasn't. You can have what's left in the pan."

"He always gets more. You always give him everything."

"Don't start, okay? Please?"

"But it's true."

"You're just upset. Finish eating now and let's—"

"No!" He throws his spoon down. It bounces off his bowl to the floor, scattering macaroni and cheese everywhere.

I draw a deep breath.

Louie slips off his chair and scurries, hands over ears, to his room.

"Can't you ever just eat, John? For Christ's sake, can't you ever just eat?"

"Like a normal person," my father says to me. "Not like some goddamn animal. A dog or a pig, whatever. *They* lick off of plates. We don't. You understand me?" *Sir! Yes, sir, I understand you, sir!* "And don't look at me like that, son. That's exactly what got you in trouble in the first place—that go-to-hell look of yours. Someday it's going to get you knocked ass over appetite. Make what happened at dinner seem like a picnic. Mark my word."

He turns away.

I turn away from John displaying a mouthful of half-chewed macaroni and cheese.

14   *Glimmer Train Stories*

Our eyes meet, my father's and mine.

And that could be it. That could be the end right there, everything coming 'round in a neat circle—me sitting at the table with *my* son now, seeing what I'm seeing, thinking what I'm thinking—a scene destined to be played over and over, generation after generation.

But that isn't it.

What I'd like to say instead is that we have a long heart-to-heart talk, a real conversation in which we iron out our differences forever and ever. After that, we take a nice after-dinner stroll through the neighborhood, stopping on our way home for ice cream, then take baths and get ready for bed without complaining.

But that isn't it either.

"Papa?" John says after a while, hand stretched across the table to touch my arm. "Want to play baseball?"

"Yeah, want to?" says Louie, returning to drink his milk.

"I get to bat first," John says.

"Me," Louie says.

"All right," John says. "I'll catch. After you get three outs, I bat."

"Okay."

"Want to then, Papa?" They're looking at me, half-smiling, nodding. "Come on, please? Say you want to."

Mary Ellis

This is my brother, Paul, and me, eating watermelon (the dog is, too). I loved and ate so much watermelon and cantaloupe as a kid that my uncle Doc nicknamed me Melon Butt. Summer meant melons to me, not only because they are abundant during that season, but because I thought that if I could taste the sun, it would taste just like that explosion of deep orange musky-sweetness contained in a cantaloupe.

Mary Ellis was born and raised in northern Wisconsin and educated at the University of Minnesota. Her fiction has appeared in the *Wisconsin Academy Review*, the *Milwaukee Journal's Sunday Magazine*, the *Bellingham Review*, *Glimmer Train Stories*, and most recently in the anthology *Uncommon Waters: Women Write about Fishing* (Seal Press).

MARY ELLIS
Angel

Of course we have had our differences which at times turned into bitter arguments; then I would bite my lip so as to not cry out. That is natural, human: love is a series of scars. "No heart is as whole as a broken heart," said the celebrated Rabbi Nahman of Bratzlav.

—Elie Wiesel, *The Fifth Son*

angel (ānj́əl) n. 2. A guardian spirit or guiding influence
5. *Military.* Enemy aircraft

—*American Heritage Dictionary*

Ernie Morriseau knew the exact moment that Jimmy Lucas had died.

It was late January in 1969. The sunset had been an unusually spectacular orange-red, like the sunsets of late summer, and was streaked with clouds shaped like scattered fleece. He had been shoveling manure for about an hour behind the barn, adding to the pile already banked up against the outside wall, when he stopped to have a smoke and ponder the sunset. Northern Wisconsin had been experiencing a freak midwinter thaw and the temperatures during the day had reached the low forties for the past week. But now dusk was rapidly taking over and the temperature was dropping. Ernie put out his cigarette and hurried to get the job done because in another half hour he wouldn't be able to see or feel his hands on the shovel. As he worked, he could hear the family dog inspecting and exploring through the thick wet snow around the barn.

Ernie was straining to lift an enormous shovelful when he heard the dog stop prowling and give a quick snort. Thinking the dog had just found an unlucky mouse under the snow, Ernie tossed the manure onto the pile and was about to shovel up some more when he realized that the dog had stopped moving completely. He straightened up and was trying to locate the dog when he heard him instead. A long, high howl broke the farmyard quiet. Ernie shivered and involuntarily dropped the shovel. Then the dog streaked right past him, jumping over the shovel and running about three hundred yards into the snow-crusted field behind the barn. Ernie turned in the direction the dog had taken, wondering what had spooked him, when he saw that the large black animal had stopped again and stood rigidly still with his head and nose held high. He looked beyond the dog and that was when he saw Jimmy Lucas.

At first, Ernie thought that Jimmy had been discharged early from the army and was finally home from fighting in Vietnam. But he was wearing his combat helmet and fatigues, and carrying a rifle. Ernie stepped forward, sinking into the snow, and raised his arm.

"Jimmy!" he yelled and waved his hand.

Jimmy Lucas didn't answer and instead reached up and took off his helmet, dropping it into the snow. The helmet rolled as though it had hit hard ground instead of snow and Ernie noticed that Jimmy was standing on top of the snow instead of sinking into it as Ernie and the dog had. Suddenly Ernie knew it was and wasn't Jimmy Lucas, and why he was standing in the Morriseaus' eighty-acre field behind the barn. Ernie sank to his knees.

"Oh no, Jimmy," he whispered. "No, no Jimmy."

As Ernie watched, Jimmy dropped his rifle, too, and slowly turned around. The dog snorted again but did not move. Then Jimmy walked away from them and continued walking until he reached the big swamp that bordered the Morriseau and Lucas farms. The very moment that Jimmy disappeared into the

18   *Glimmer Train Stories*

swamp, the dog howled again and took off running, floundering through the snow until he, too, reached the swamp.

An hour went by before Ernie was able to rise to his feet. He threw the shovel into the toolshed and reluctantly approached the house. Methodically and silently he ate dinner before trudging up the stairs to bed. Thinking it was exhaustion, his wife only asked where the dog was, and didn't question her husband's decision to go to sleep early.

Two days later the official news came. James Lucas had been killed in action in an unspecified location near the DMZ.

It's July. The dog lies on the porch, catching the hot July wind in his mouth, tasting it between his pink tongue and the roof of his mouth before panting it out again. I watch him determine in a second what the messages are in the wind—who's coming, who's been where, who's alive, who's dead—and then he sends his own message when he lets the wind go, to whatever animal will savor and understand it as he does. Angel's done this a million times. He's an old dog. So I imagine he has much to say.

I'm washing the supper dishes, listening to some old records, watching the dog, and ignoring the heat. The records are stacked like a vinyl layer cake, losing a layer every time a record falls and is played on the stereo. Right now, Roy Orbison is singing one of my favorite songs. "Blue Angel."

"Hey!" I yell, rapping the kitchen window with a soapy knuckle. "He's singing your song."

Angel briefly looks up at me, and then, swatting a horsefly away from his mangled ear with his front paw, resumes his panting. I stare at the dog, stretched out on the porch floor. And I remember the day we found him twelve years ago.

We were driving home from a Friday night fish fry when I thought I saw something moving in the shadows beside the road. Ernie slowed the truck down. I motioned for him to stop and rolled down my window.

Something big and dark was trying to drag itself back into the ditch, away from the headlights. At first I thought it was a bear cub and looked up at the trees along the road for the sow. Ernie opened his door and stepped out. Then he stood there, leaning against the open door and taking long drags on his cigarette. I waited. My husband continued to just stare at the ditch. Finally, I leaned over in the seat.

"Are you meditating or what? You want me to check it out?" I whispered.

Ernie dropped his cigarette and smashed it with the heel of his boot.

"Wait a minute," he said. "I think it's a dog."

He slowly walked around the front of the truck and to the edge of the ditch. I poked my head out of the window just in time to hear a low growl. My scalp tingled.

"Be careful! He might have rabies," I whispered again, and grabbed the flashlight out of the glove compartment. I got out of the truck and shined the light down into the ditch.

Ernie was right. There, in the watery mud of spring, was a dog, his breath whistling through his blood-caked nose. He was about six months old but was already a big animal. The light caught the glistening blood running down the side of his head and he weakly pulled himself around so that he faced us. He was as black as a night without stars. Blue-black. One eye shined white and luminous in the light but the other was swollen shut and covered with clotting blood. Ernie stepped forward for a better look. The dog barked and tried to lunge forward.

"Christ!" Ernie said, stepping back. "It looks like he's been shot in the head and shot in his left hip...and I think he caught some buckshot in his chest. Whoever it was couldn't shoot straight. That's why he's still alive...and in one piece. Good-lookin' dog though, huh Rose? Think he's part Lab?"

The dog looked away from Ernie and focused on me with his one good eye before I could answer. I stared at that dog. He stared at me. His eye burned a path through all the hidden memories in my head. Standing on that dusky gravel road, I felt the sudden chill of knowing what the reality of his wounds meant. The same meaning that accompanies a calf born too deformed to live, or a piglet whose back has been broken by the carelessness of its mother's bulky roll in the pen. It is not a mean decision but one that comes with the harshness of rural life and expensive veterinarian bills. Ernie had anticipated what was coming and had already retrieved the shotgun from the back of the truck. I ignored the gun and squatted, resting on the balls of my feet.

"You're right. Looks like almost all Lab. Poor fella," I crooned.

He stopped growling and whimpered. Then Ernie cautiously moved toward him again. His good eye left me and zeroed in on Ernie. He growled, this time baring his teeth. That's how I knew it was a man that shot him and threw him into that ditch. His head must have been searing with pain, like someone stuck a knife into it, but he could still tell a woman from a man.

I loved him in that instant.

"Nope," I said. "Not this time. I can fix him up."

"Oh Lord, Rose," Ernie said. "It's pretty bad. He's never gonna be the same. He's gotta be in a helluva lot of pain, too."

I started to get up and prepare myself for a good fight with

Ernie. But as I stood up, a sudden warm infused me from my belly up to my chest that felt almost blessed. I am not a religious person but I can't think of any other way to describe it. It was like that circular feeling I had when I anticipated being a mother and remembered what it was like to be mothered; that feeling of having been chosen without having to ask. And this dog chose me.

"Well?" my husband asked, turning to face me. Then the name just popped into my head.

"Angel," I said. "We're going to take him home and call him Angel."

"Angel?" Ernie said, giving me a funny look. "He looks more like a Bruno to me."

"Angel," I repeated.

Ernie shrugged and walked to the bed of the truck for some twine. Angel's good ear stood up like a small wing. I kept talking to him until he slumped back into the mud. He gazed into the flashlight beam and became mesmerized enough by both the pain and the light so that Ernie could grab his muzzle, tying the twine around it so he wouldn't bite us. Then we took him home.

I don't know how he lived. Whoever tried to blow his brains out missed the best part, the telling part. Angel has fits every now and then, chasing his tail around and around, and sometimes he gallops in his sleep, his legs scissoring through the air and going nowhere. His head appears a little lopsided when you look at him straight on, and the shredded remains of his one ear wave in the breeze. They are soft though, when you touch them, like strips of black chamois cloth. He let me touch him from the very beginning. But it took Angel a long time to trust Ernie. I've always been secretly proud that Angel took to me right off. I'm good with animals and children, but Ernie's better.

Angel's memory is whole and enduring. I don't think any of the buckshot got into that part of his brain even though I can feel with my fingertips the round bumps of lead coming to the surface when I rub his head. When he loves, he loves completely, recognizing someone he trusts even after years of not seeing them. He lopes down the driveway in an easy way, his big tongue hanging out. This is the way he greets women and children. Yet his hatred is just as complete, just as absolute. He hates men, all men, except for Ernie and our neighbor Bill Lucas and his brother Jimmy; even though Bill's a grown man now and not the little boy who spent so much time visiting us; even though Jimmy's been dead for twelve years, bombed into a hillside in Vietnam.

Angel's my dog. He sits in the cab of the truck with his big muzzle poking out of the window, tasting the wind as we fly down the road.

I'm almost done with the dishes. It's seven o'clock, it's hotter than hell, and I've got the blues really bad. I look out of the window in the hope that I'll think of something else besides crying when a flash of color catches my eye from the Lucas field. Then I see Bill Lucas, tall and hunched, walking along the edge of the field that borders the big swamp and our field. Angel sees him too and scrambles to his feet. His good ear rises like a flag, but he doesn't bark.

"There goes your friend," I say softly, but of course the dog can't hear me through the window.

Bill stops then. Just stops and stands there and faces the big swamp. Angel continues to silently watch him. He lifts his nose. I turn my head for just a minute and that's when Angel barks, once. I look back just in time to see Bill get swallowed into the thick cover of those swamp cedars. This is the fifth time this summer I've seen him disappear like that into the swamp. I stand up on my toes to catch a glimpse of him but he's gone and the only thing I see now is my husband by the toolshed, watching Bill just like me, just like the dog.

Once last summer I saw Bill up close at the Standard station where he works, and was shocked by the oily stubble and savage look of his face. His eyes are no longer the soft gray color they were when he was a kid. They are a rock gray now, and like a split rock they are small but with jagged edges.

We wait and watch, but nothing. Ernie's shoulders sag when he realizes that Bill will not reappear and he trudges off toward the barn, sixty years of exhaustion in every step.

We will not talk about this. My husband does not know that I know he watches the Lucas place, looking for signs of life— a vigorous wave of a hand or the yellow halo of the yard light when night falls. The little boy who used to visit our farm, eat dinner with us, and play with the dog has grown into a remote and painfully shy young man. We see him rarely and almost always at a distance. And the oddest thing is that his name is never spoken between us...as though he were dead instead of his brother Jimmy. Which is nonsense because we do *see him*, working, walking, or driving, even if it isn't often. It hurts Ernie that Bill does not come to our place anymore or accept visits easily from us. But Ernie doesn't talk about that either. He deals with his pain like most men, treating it as though it doesn't exist, and therefore, cannot be talked about.

I, on the other hand, have never been known to stay quiet. When I'm in pain I cry a blue streak, and when I'm angry I yell like hell. And when something is bothering me, I talk. A lot.

But I don't have another person to talk to easily outside of Ernie, who's been punishing me with silence for the past two weeks, and who has even struggled to keep his feet from touching mine while we sleep. I don't even know what I'm being punished for, that's how nonexistent our conversations have been. I've given up trying, fearful that I might use the most intimate details that people who have lived together for a long time can carry like swords. But I still need to talk to somebody. Most of our neighbors are a good two, three miles away and busy farmers like us. So I talk to the dog whose eyes have taken on a kind of old-man wisdom to match his graying muzzle.

Some days it's hilarious. Angel patiently trails behind me as I do the housework, ducking behind a chair when I vacuum, sitting by the bathroom door as I scrub the toilet and floor, or lying on the porch while I peel vegetables or count eggs, all the while listening to the constant run of my mouth.

It is only at night when I let Angel out of the house that he leaves me for a few hours, running out the door and into the nearest patch of woods with the determination of a reconnaissance pilot, his black coat giving him a natural camouflage at night. In the past I had only an inkling of what he did on these forays; what any male dog would do, and him especially, pent up all day in the house with me. But lately I've suspected that Angel's nightly journeys are not meaningless wanderings or chance matings, and if he could talk he would tell me things that my husband never does. It frightens me. Other women who are isolated and lonely drink or pick fights with their silent husbands, or take up with other men, or maybe just suffer silently. I talk to the dog. And watch a little boy who was never mine and who has long since grown up and abandoned me.

Then this morning at breakfast my husband, who has borne like a Buddhist monk the hardships of being a WW II veteran, a farmer, and a mixed-blood man in northern Wisconsin, did talk to me, only to hurt me. He put down his coffee cup and said, "I just can't do it anymore, Rose. I used to be able to lift a bale of hay in each hand, and now I can barely lift one with two hands. I can't sleep worth a shit, and things that used to mean so much to me don't anymore. I just don't give a damn."

What could I say? For other people the meaning of life does not rest on being able to lift a bale of hay. But we're farmers. Everything rests on that bale of hay. Actually, it was the look on his face, not what Ernie said, that did me in this morning. The message was loudly broadcast with those dark brown, bloodshot, and tired eyes. That bale of hay should have been passed onto younger hands. We are Rosemary and Ernest Morriseau—good farmers, but farmers *without children*.

I sat as though slapped speechless. My lips moved but no sound came out. Ernie stood up as though he didn't notice, maybe he didn't care, and walked out the kitchen door.

I give a damn, is what I couldn't spit out. *I tried*. And it got worse as the day went on. I could barely keep my head up, could barely talk for fear of tears.

Now the dishes are done and the dog is scratching at the door to be let in. I open the door and Angel strolls through the doorway, his nails tapping like drumsticks on the linoleum. Then he sits and looks up at me, my only friend.

Suddenly I can't look at the dog and I can't breathe. I stumble out of the kitchen and into the living room, but Angel trails me. When I reach for, and slump into, the old brown recliner by the window, I am temporarily relieved of the burden of Ernie's words, of Ernie's silence. I cry, hiccuping and sputtering like a three-year-old. I cry for hours until it gets dark, until my eyes become puffy and my head aches. Angel rubs his scarred head against my knee for a while before settling down next to the chair. I'm grateful for even that amount of touch.

I love this dog and this dog loves me. But when did my husband and I stop doing the dance of love? What have I done, what crime have I committed that warrants being ignored? That justifies not being touched? And when will I stop being punished, however slightly, for the children I could not give birth to?

I met Ernie at a Legion party in Milwaukee. I was an army nurse who had just finished my tour of duty in the Philippines, and Ernie was a shrapnel-filled soldier. I was sipping my favorite drink of depression, a gin and tonic, and spiraling downward when I smelled cedar. I turned around to stare into a pair of the most velvety brown eyes I'd ever seen. He had a chest like a gladiator and hair the color of my most recent dreams. Black. But his voice was warm and soft.

"War's over. Wanna dance?" he asked, and smiled that enormous slow smile that made me put down my drink, suddenly crazed to wrap my arms around that huge, cedar-smelling chest and hold on for as long as I could.

We both held on like two long-lost buddies from childhood. He was from northern Wisconsin like me. We got married and left Milwaukee to take on his family farm in Olina. Then I tried having babies.

The doctor said my uterus was damaged but he couldn't figure out how. I told him that I'd been sick, on and off, in the Philippines with what was thought to be some kind of intestinal flu.

"Well," he commented nonchalantly, "maybe that did it," and motioned for me to get dressed. Then he said to quit trying. But I tried.

Just when I would start to think that this one was going to hold, and get ready to shop for baby clothes, I'd feel that damn ache in my lower back. Then the contractions would come on fast, and before I could get to the hospital twenty miles away, my lovely baby would slip and fall out, looking like clotted peony petals shaken from the stem into a pool of blood.

I remember the last baby. I was in the bathroom, feeling that downward pull and squeezing my thighs together to hold it in.

"Don't leave me. Don't leave me," I kept saying. Chanting it, Ernie said, long after the baby was gone and he'd taken me to the hospital. Ernie had been kind enough after the first three miscarriages. But as they continued, he made love to me as though he were pouring precious seed onto waterless ground.

Then Ernie and I got two sons by default, at least for a short time, and my husband and the ghosts of our own children were temporarily appeased. First Jimmy and then Bill began to visit us, driven out of their house by their father's rageful drinking and their mother's mental descent into another world. I didn't give a damn about Jon Lucas, but Claire was like too many women I'd seen and grown up with. Women with brains three times the size and depth of their fathers' and husbands', but trapped and nowhere to go with that kind of intelligence but sideways or down. I tried for a long time to get close to Claire, but she avoided me as though I were painful to her. I used to watch her walk in one continuous circle around the edge of their back forty acres while Jimmy was in the army and Billy was at school, her hands talking to the air, and her face slanted toward the sky.

"She's losing it," I said to Ernie once when we watched her discreetly from behind our barn.

"You don't know that for sure," my husband said, surprising me. "Maybe she really is talking to someone."

"Do you see anybody else out there?" I asked sarcastically.

"I'm just sayin' there's alotta things we don't know about," Ernie answered and shrugged.

"Especially in that family," I cracked, and even Ernie had to nod.

But I felt lousy saying it and shut up after that, not wanting to tempt the spirits. *There but for the grace of God*, I thought, *go I*. I rationalized it away, thinking that Claire probably needed a break from the kids, and opened up our house and my arms to Jimmy and Bill, letting the love pour. But that was not enough. Jimmy became a teenager so hell-bent on escaping his old man that enlisting in the army looked like a sure chance in a million-dollar lottery in comparison to his life in Olina. Then Jimmy lost the lottery. In her grief, Claire Lucas woke up and realized that she had another son, keeping little Bill close to home after that. And Ernie and I lost both of them. I don't know who I cried more for, Ernie and I, or Jimmy and Bill.

Then when Bill was sixteen, his father died of a heart attack. I could not find any warmth in that kid's hand when I shook it after the funeral mass. It was as though he didn't know or remember me. But the look on his face was one that couldn't be mistaken. While Claire appeared bewildered and exhausted, her son was obviously relieved instead of sad.

"You'd be relieved too! He won't have that stinkin' mean drunk for a father anymore," Ernie commented bitterly on the drive home.

When Bill turned eighteen, he inherited the farm and Claire gratefully moved to a small house across from the church in Olina, becoming a receptionist for the Forest Service. She seems much better now but she still won't accept my friendship.

I'm almost ready to drift off to sleep when I hear the steps creak. Angel wakes up and cocks his head toward the staircase. I wait and watch. My husband's shuffling body fills the doorway. He is wearing what he always wears to bed, a pair of blue pajama bottoms and nothing else. It's too dark for me to see his face, but I know something is wrong by the way his big shoulders are slumped forward.

"You know," he begins quietly, "my grandma Morriseau told me before I was shipped out to the Pacific that I would know if anyone close to me had died. Here at home or over there. I told her I didn't wanna know. She said, want to or not, I would just know, especially if I kept my mind open to it. I thought it was just old Indian superstition. Nothin' ever happened during my service that made me think about what she said. Except my buddy, Frank. His old French-Canadian, Catholic mother told him almost the same thing. We laughed about it."

I'm either so tired or it's really been a strange day. This morning he tells me he doesn't care anymore, and now it's almost midnight and he's telling me about his reservation grandmother who's been dead for almost thirty years.

"But," he says, his voice dropping an octave, "I had a bad feeling when Jimmy left for basic training."

MARY ELLIS

I am instantly wide awake.

"*Jimmy?*" I ask. "What about Jimmy?"

Ernie went on as though he didn't hear what I said.

"I didn't pay any attention to it," he says. "I figured I felt that way because of the kind of war it was. But when I saw him, I knew I had done a bad thing. I could've invited him over to dinner with Billy that night, remember? Before he shipped out the next day? But I didn't 'cause of what he did to that turtle with that stupid-ass Schwartz kid he used to hang out with. I could've went after him, talked to him about what he was getting himself into. I could've talked him out of it. I came so close," he says and then repeats, "so close."

"Ernie," I say. "Don't you remember? We didn't know that Jimmy had even enlisted until that night Billy came over for dinner. Remember when Jon came over to pick up Billy, he told us. Remember you were so mad because Jon was *proud* of it, and you said he was just getting rid of his son before the kid took him down. Don't you remember?"

"I *saw* Jimmy," he says, his voice dropping to a whisper, "two days before we heard about him. Remember, it was so warm that winter? I was shoveling manure. Well...that's when I saw him. Angel," he gestures toward the dog, "saw him first and howled like crazy. Jimmy was standing in the back field. But he didn't say a word, not a word. He just took off his helmet and dropped his gun. Then," Ernie swallows, "he turned around and walked into the swamp. That's when I knew...that Jimmy had died."

My husband, by nature, does not exaggerate. Still, I find his words hard to believe until I remember that Ernie didn't cry like I did when we heard the news. At the time, I thought it was because he had accepted it as a consequence of war. He'd fought. He knew the chances. Now it all makes sense. For the past twelve years, he has been trudging through his daily life, not silenced by hard solitary work, but by grief.

"I wanted to tell you," he says, suddenly shaking so much that the air seems to crack around him. "Then this morning when I saw the look on your face...so lonely, *so lonely*, it hit me what a goddamn bastard I've been. I'm sorry, Rose. I'm so sorry."

Then Ernie covers his face with his hands, and hunching over, lets out a long, deep sob that echoes through the room. My heart hits the wall of my chest.

I don't remember the last time Ernie cried. It must have been years ago. I've cried plenty and I've heard lots of other women cry, too. But women cry, even in their worst pain, with hope and relief. They cry like wolves and coyotes do, howling to talk to their mates as well as to the rest of the pack. But there is something about the way men cry that sounds so hopeless, so anguished, as though the very act of crying is killing them.

I could feel the tears start up fresh in my eyes.

"C'mere," I say, and open my arms to stop the waters.

My husband stumbles toward me. The recliner moans under our weight as Ernie sinks into my arms. Angel bolts up and trots over by the TV. He hunkers down in front of it, alert but oddly calm. He lifts his nose to sniff the air, then opens his mouth to taste it. Our big black dog, satisfied with what his nose and tongue read, lowers his lopsided head to rest in a pool of moonlight on the floor. I wrap my arms tighter around Ernie, touching with my fingertips the scars and pointed shrapnel still under his skin. He nuzzles his face deep into the crook of my neck to hide it while he cries.

I wish there were some way I could tell Jimmy that Ernie cries for him. I wonder if Jon Lucas ever grieved so for what was his flesh-and-blood son. We thought not at the time. He'd brag in town about Jimmy being a war hero and tell stories as though he'd actually been there with Jimmy, fighting in the jungle. Ernie and the other veterans in town never talked like that. They'd done it. They knew war wasn't a movie. It was hell personified, and for them to talk about it was to give it new life, to raise the dead. And I covered up so many shattered bodies in the hospital in the Philippines that I had dreams. Terrible dreams that lasted for twenty years. I dreamt that my limbs were being torn off or that I was being shot into the air by the force of an exploding bomb, or that I was being held at gunpoint, unable to speak Japanese, and finally, being bayoneted through the chest. My worst dream, though, was of a large white sheet descending on me from above, and I was still alive and fighting to keep that endless white cotton from smothering me. Jon Lucas just couldn't know. Whatever it was that made him drink, it wasn't the crap of war.

The dog exhales a deep lungful of air, but his eyes stay open, luminescent in the white light. I stare at him until I realize that I have forgotten to let him out for his nightly wandering. Then it dawns on me that he has not made the slightest familiar sign of wanting to go outside.

My head suddenly clears from years of shameful and cloudy debris, and my skin prickles.

Oh yes, I want to say out loud. *Yes, yes, yes.*

Grandma Morriseau was right about such things.

Up until now, I would've traded Angel to have had at least one child come out of my rickety womb. I was at one of the lowest points in my life when we found Angel lying in that ditch. I believed, since the first time I saw him all shot up, and spared him an early death, that I had saved him. That all my stored-up and unused maternal love and care could at least save him, a mere dog. I was *determined* to save him. But all the tears in the world can't hide the truth.

If anyone was saved, it was me.

When I have given and given and danced with love until I am exhausted, when my husband remained as silent, and some days, as bitter and brittle, as a winter's day, this dog has given to me. When I have felt fragile and vulnerable; when I have wondered if Ernie would still fight for me and over me, over an aging, fifty-seven-year-old farm wife instead of the once svelte and long-legged beauty that I was, it is Angel who sits beside me in the cab of the truck while I sell eggs to homes on some of the worst back roads in this county. It is Angel who guards the farm and me from aggressive salesmen, from all the possible evil that people are capable of bestowing out of the blue. It is Angel who has kept me from talking to the air like Claire Lucas, and whose very presence has kept at a distance the haunting ghosts of my never-born children. It is Angel who circles the perimeter of the farm at night, black and mysterious, who tastes the wind and listens for sounds that we cannot hear. And it was Angel who saw Jimmy Lucas first, and who I suspect, because I will never really know, is able to talk to Bill Lucas because Ernie and I cannot. It is this big, black, scarred-up dog lying in front of us that has carried for years a spirit that is not his own.

My husband has stopped crying but makes no move to uncoil himself from my arms. Someday I will tell Ernie what I know, that it was a good thing, not a bad thing, that he saw Jimmy. That Jimmy chose him. That we cannot save anyone. That we choose to be saved ourselves.

Love, I will tell my silent husband, is never wasted.

And I will tell him, looking at Angel now sleeping by the TV, that we have never been alone.

Robert Abel

I wish I could remember this far back—fifty-one years. I figure my dad had just come home from work, or maybe he was working second shift then and was about to leave. He held that curious object just a little far away—to make me reach for it.

Robert Abel is a recent winner of the Flannery O'Connor Award for Short Fiction, and current works in print are *Ghost Traps* (University of Georgia Press) and *Full-tilt Boogie and Other Stories* (Lynx House Press).

ROBERT H. ABEL
Prized Possessions

M rs. Leola DePardo was sitting at the kitchen table reading the real estate transfers when her husband, Hank, barged through the door. He was in his fishing waders and they were wet, but he gave a "Don't say nothin'" look, grabbed one of her prized maple dining chairs, and clomped down into the basement with it.

Leola couldn't imagine what possessed Hank just then, but she continued reading, shocked to see that the Deslisle family had sold off forty acres of beautiful waterfront to that sleazeball developer, Peter Dominico. The news was shocking enough that it cooled off her irritation with Hank for tromping across her clean floor in his wet waders, something he knew by now was a family taboo. But Hank had given her such a wild look that she was temporarily disarmed. And what the hell did he need the chair for? Sometimes you could just not tell what was going through the lunatic minds of men.

In a moment she heard that damned power saw razzing— *zing, zing, zing, zing*—four times. Here she had been looking forward to a nice quiet night with Hank out fishing, and he was downstairs sawing in his wet waders. By God, if he was using her good kitchen chair to saw wood on, holding it down with those damned sandy wet wader boots, she would just kill him. She heard his electric drill buzz a few times and then Hank came clomping up the stairs again, and he went straight past her, fast, and out the door with what looked like some chunks of wood in his hands. He didn't even close the damned door behind him! Cool October air poured in through the screen—Hank hadn't put any of the storms up yet—and Leola reached behind her and swung the door shut with a slam of annoyance.

Having done whatever damned thing he did, Hank had not even bothered to return her chair to the kitchen. Leola slapped the paper down on the table and descended the basement steps to retrieve her chair. She thought she had better do this before it became a permanent fixture in Hank's workshop. She had bought the dining ensemble at an auction at one of the old Warrens' Bay estates some years ago and it was among her prized possessions, which she had a hell of a time defending against the multitudinous ways of thoughtless abuse that Hank could find to give it.

Hank—of course—had left the light on, so as soon as Leola came into the workshop she saw the unimaginable horror right there in plain view. At first she couldn't believe it, but when she did, she gave out a whimper of despair and outrage. There, in a little pool of yellow sawdust, was her kitchen chair, all four legs cut off right to the bottom spindle, about six or eight inches butchered away, and there the chair lay, on its back, so that the fresh-cut little circles of wood stared up at her like the blank whites of a murder victim's eyes. Leola stepped over to the chair and lifted it tenderly, then threw it down in disgust.

"Goddamn it, Hank!" she cried, and then growled in frustration, misery, fury. Why, why, she wondered, does a man come home in the middle of the night and saw up a beautiful kitchen chair, then disappear into the darkness? Was there anyone in Warrens' Bay, except Hank, who wouldn't regard such behavior as certifiably insane? My God, she thought, that chair was over 150 years old and could not be matched anywhere, except by the three others around the table now. They had all been handcrafted by a furniture and cabinet maker long since dead but whose skills were legendary in Warrens' Bay and, for that matter, in all of New England. If Leola told folks she had a "Grumman dining set," they would reply, "Grumman, really? How did you get your hands on that?" or "Leola, how could you ever afford such a thing?" Leola had paid 250 dollars for the set back in 1965, and now each chair alone was worth that much, if not more. But it wasn't only the money part. Why didn't Hank just come home and cut off her hand or something—what the hell was the difference? Didn't he know? She wondered again what could cause a man to behave with such reckless disregard.

And she was afraid she knew the answer to that already, at least partially. Whatever it was, it had something to do with fishing. It just made her tired. Wasn't there anything in the world besides striped bass? Anything at all? Like, for example, antique Grumman dining ensembles? Couldn't Hank understand anything besides fishing? That look in his eyes when he came through the door, really, Leola thought, you'd have thought he was on drugs. She trudged up the stairs to the kitchen and surveyed the Grumman survivors, wondering if she should hide the other chairs away or if that would just cause Hank to carve up the table for some reason. She moaned in despair and anger. Wasn't Hank going to get a piece of her mind when he got back! Sawing the legs off a Grumman chair! Jesus, Hank! Sometimes you make me mad enough to kill!

She sat and read again the Deslisle sale to Dominico. Such a beautiful beach meadow going over to tourist condos sometime soon. It miffed her. You wouldn't think the Deslisles would need to sell any land, she thought. They seemed pretty well off, comparatively. And *that* land, of all their land, which sloped down to a beautiful rocky beach, where Hank said he had caught some nice bass not very long ago, which he sold for good money. Would Dominico change that, too, haul off the rocks and bring in sand? Post the beach and get the fishermen up in flames? Warrens' Bay was changing too fast, Leola thought. She also thought maybe a quota on New Yorkers and Bostonians would be a good thing, if you could just enforce it. They were driving the prices of everything right out of sight for the people who live here year-round. If they hated the city so much, why the hell were they working so hard to turn Warrens' Bay into one? Imagine anyone living here trying to buy one of those beach condos. The idea of a bulldozer charging into those dunes made Leola sick. But there it was. Right in the paper. That little notice was going to be good for a hundred hours of rancorous debate at town meeting, surely. Jesus! Did everything have to get spoiled?

Leola was working herself into a fine, if frustrating, frenzy. It's like that chair, she thought; it's done—it can't be fixed, so why agitate myself into an early grave. So my husband is stupid and insensitive sometimes, I guess I chose to marry him, and we've had good times, we've made out, a little on the shaky side, but hey. They said "for better or for worse" but they didn't say, "Suppose he cuts up one of your prized possessions one night," did they? Still, Hank wasn't going to get off scot-free. She was sick about that chair and she was going to let Hank know it.

The clock over the kitchen sink where the supper dishes were piled and sparkling, "air drying," as Hank called it—"I'll just let them air dry tonight, Babe, okay?"—said it was almost midnight, and Leola gave up the idea of calling anyone to vent her complaints. It had long since proved fruitless to call Hank's father, not because he was ever insensitive, but just because he had become so strange and unpredictable lately, thanks to the onset of Alzheimer's disease. Leola's mother, too, was going to bed awfully early now, nine or nine-thirty; and her friend Gracie was still working tables at the Hook Nook until it closed down for the season in a week or so. The locals didn't pay much attention to the Hook Nook, and so it closed in the winter, and

38   *Glimmer Train Stories*

then Leola saw Gracie almost every day. She would love to show Gracie the chair in the basement right now, just as it lay there, just say, "Come here, Gracie. I want to show you something." Just take her down there and turn on the light. She knew what Gracie would say.

"Holy shit, Leola! He didn't!"

Leola would grimace and nod.

Gracie would grab her hair in her hands and turn to Leola with her mouth agape and she would say, "And he's still alive?"

At two-thirty in the morning, Hank had still not come home, and Leola had carried her anger around for so long that it just melted into disgust and she went to bed. Alone, she was cold and didn't sleep well, and when she woke up at five o'clock and Hank still wasn't there, she began to get worried. That'd be just like him, she thought, cut up my chair and then drown himself, too. She heard him talk one night, over beers in the kitchen with his fishing pals, about how he had waded at low tide out to fish the channel at Crimp's Light and then got trapped on the bar by the incoming tide because he had stayed there too late and might have been washed right off in his waders except that the caretaker on the island there had seen him and putted out in a dinghy. Because he and the caretaker both hadn't wanted to risk tipping the little boat, Hank had had to hold onto the gunwale and be towed like that back to the beach. Oh, they had all laughed and banged their beers on the Grumman table, but Leola had thought, that fool might just have disappeared, and where would that leave me? She wondered now if Hank could do such a stupid thing twice, and in the dark, and she knew, yeah, damn right he could. Him and his "one more cast." And then one more. Oh, and one more. And one more. Yes, he could trap himself again like that if he thought he had the scantiest chance of hooking a big bass there.

Maybe I'd better go look, she thought. I'll go down to Tina's anyway, have a coffee, ask some questions. Somebody down there will have seen him someplace. I got to look up Dan Grey anyway one of these days, see if he's hiring any scallop shuckers sometime soon. She dressed quickly and went out into the cool morning. The grass beaded with drops and the sky toward the ocean was a deep, watery blue above a fluorescent orange band of sunrise. Along the road to Tina's Diner were thick patches of fog that incandesced in her headlights.

Inside Tina's there were only two old-timers at the counter, the Compte brothers, Earl and Jake, passing sections of the newspaper back and forth. Tina herself was leaning against the counter, her silver hair glowing in the overhead lights, but she began pouring a coffee for Leola as soon as she came in the door.

"Hello, Leola, where you been so long?"

"Pretty quiet in here this morning, ain't it?" Leola took the coffee in both hands to warm them up.

"Everybody's on the beach," Tina said. "I'm surprised you haven't heard. You and the Comptes here and me are about the only people in town not fishing right now."

Earl Compte looked over at Tina and Leola, and pulled down his glasses. "Me and Jake don't care if we never see another fish," he said.

"What beach?" Leola asked.

"I heard they been moving right along from Black Rocks right out to North Head. They say it's a big blitz. Bass and bluefish. They got a mess of menhaden trapped right on the beach and are even coming into the bay after them. That's what they tell me. Guys been coming in here so tired from catching fish they can't walk."

"I guess that's why I ain't seen Hank."

"You might go down to the fish house if you want to make some spending money," Tina said. "They'll be swamped with fish pretty soon."

"I had enough fish in this life to last me," Earl Compte

40   *Glimmer Train Stories*

interjected. "You see what's sitting here on my plate, don't you? Sausages. You can take those kippers and fling 'em. I don't care if there's a million bass out there right now. As for bluefish—to me, they're the same as flies."

Headlights flashed across the diner window and Leola turned to see who was pulling up, hoping to see Hank. In a moment Billy Harper came through the door, old blue baseball cap to his eyebrows, his waders jiggling. He was so tired he had bags under his eyes that made him look ten years older than his forty-five years.

"Don't come in here in those waders," Tina said. "Can't you read the sign?"

"What sign?" Billy said. This was, of course, what all the fishermen said when they came in and sat down in their waders.

"And they wonder why they get parking tickets," Tina said to Leola. "Don't let him sit next to you, either, those old waders smell like a clam flats."

"Billy Harper can sit next to me anytime," Leola said, teasing.

Billy did, in fact, sit next to Leola, though he left an empty stool between them. He was not a big man and the gesture struck Leola as both self-conscious and polite. His wife had died five years ago now and he still hadn't remarried, he was so shy or so hurt still, or both. Before he could open his mouth, however, Earl Compte asked him how the fishing was.

"Oh, you'd love it out there," Billy said. "A bass on every cast. It's been a dream night and a dream morning."

"I'm glad I'm right here where it's warm," Earl insisted.

"We've got to get 'em while we can, Earl. You know they're going to regulate bass fishing pretty soon now."

Billy quickly turned his attention to Leola and asked, "Have you seen Hank by any chance?"

"Not since he sawed up my chair at midnight," she said. "He's out on the beach, surely. I was going to ask you the same thing."

"Yeah, well," Billy said, looking pained, lacing his fingers together. "He must be out there somewhere."

Billy unlaced his hands and then leaned on his fist a moment before he spoke. "Well, we just come on his truck, Leola. It's in the water at a place we call Good Rip."

"Oh, for Christ's sake," Leola said. "He got stuck out there again."

"That's what we figured," Billy said. "He must've got stuck out there and came in looking for some help, and then the tide came in before he got back."

"You mean it's not just stuck," Leola said. "You mean it's under water." She felt suddenly sick.

"To tell you the goddamned truth, Leola," Billy said, looking at her with his beautiful blue, wolfish eyes, "it looks to me like it even floated some to get where it is."

"You mean," Leola said, "you don't even know if he's in that goddamned truck or not?" Her voice rose oddly.

"He didn't have any slips at the fish house just now," Billy said, "but he's probably around here someplace."

"I'm going to call the house," Leola said. "If he don't answer, Billy, will you take me out there?"

"Maybe you'd better stay here," Billy said.

"Honey, don't use the pay phone," Tina said. "Use the one in the back there. Let it ring a long time. He's probably tired as hell and sleeping sound."

There was no answer.

On the ride out into the dunes, Billy Harper told Leola about the night on the beach. The fish were everywhere and they were big, and then the bluefish moved in, too, and tackle was being busted all over the place. The surf was pretty rough until early; maybe she heard it. When Leola told Billy about Hank's coming in to carve up a chair of hers, she could see Billy suppress a smile before he speculated that Hank had transformed the chair legs into "poppers," fishing lures that floated and bobbed and made a noise to attract the fish.

"He was probably out there when just the money guys were on the blitz," Billy said, "and they wouldn't lend him any gear. Or maybe he was just by himself and didn't see anybody else. I mean, to ask for tackle."

"Or maybe he just didn't want anybody to know he was into fish or where he was into them," Leola said. "He's like that."

"Most of us are like that," Billy said. "There was lots of fog, though, too. Maybe he just didn't see anybody else he knew on the trail out."

"You think maybe the fog is why he landed in the water?"

"Maybe," Billy said. "Maybe you know there's a long bar at Good Rip that's exposed at low tide. He might have driven out there thinking he was on the beach trail still. But maybe he was just out there loading up his fish and the truck got caught in the tide. I told you it was pounding some. Maybe a couple of combers snuck in there and buried the wheels in sand before he could get the fish loaded."

"Maybe, maybe," Leola said, trying to stay calm. "But if it floated, Billy, maybe he just drove off into the channel?" The idea flooded Leola with fear, exactly, she thought, like a wave breaking over the bar. She felt like a wave broke right over her.

"Let's hope not," Billy said. He and Leola swayed in the trail ruts, almost as if they were dancing.

"Why not, Billy?"

"Do you really want to think about it?"

"Tell me why not."

"Because he'd be in his waders and it's hard to maneuver out from under the steering wheel in these things. Because the water pressure would make it damn hard to open the door. Because the current can flip you around, disorient you."

Leola saw all these things happening to Hank, saw them clearly, as in a movie. She moaned aloud.

"I'm sorry, Leola."

"Don't be. It's real."

"I know what you're going through."

"I know you do, Billy," Leola said. "I'm glad I'm with you."

When they jounced through the dunes at Good Rip, the sun was a blazing pink ball, and looking out over the water was difficult because of the intensity of the glare. Three or four fishermen were standing on the beach, their rods spiked, their trucks backed up to the dune. Hank was not among them. Leola could see now that Hank's pickup was farther out than she had imagined, and somehow stuck nose-down in the sand. The bed of the pickup was visible, awash in a pink curl of foam, and just a corner of the top of the cab, which created a long, flat glide in the current, like a rock in a stream.

One of the fishermen came up to Billy's window, and he nodded guiltily, a little sheepishly, toward Leola. The man's name was Wilson Mentor, a mechanic who had worked on Hank's and Leola's cars for many years. His hands had been under the hood of the pickup in the water now. Leola supposed it was he who had recognized it first.

"The current's still too strong to get out there and get a line on it," Wilson said.

"No need to rush," Billy said.

"I guess maybe you didn't find Hank yet."

"He'll turn up," Billy said. "How much longer till dead low?"

Leola looked away when he said this. The phrase hurt.

"We thought it'd be lower by now," Wilson said. "It's holding pretty good. Course, he's in the channel, too. I mean, the truck is. We may need a boat."

Leola stepped out of the cab and shielded her eyes against the sun. The wind was making the grass in the dunes hiss steadily.

"You want to go back to Tina's and wait?" Billy asked. "Maybe Hank's there now, having coffee and pie."

"I'm not leavin'," Leola said, but did not verbalize the rest of her thought. *Not till I see if he's inside, inside there.* She sat on the beach suddenly, in a way that might have looked petulant to

Billy and the others, but was simply required because her knees had buckled under her. In a moment, Wilson came around the truck and stood beside her. Like the others, he looked bearish and clumsy in his waders, a little alien.

"Damn shame to lose that truck," Wilson said.

"I don't care about the truck," Leola said.

"I don't think there's anything to worry about, really," Wilson said.

Leola scooped sand in her palm and let it trickle out between her fingers, saying nothing in reply. She wanted people just to shut up and stop reassuring her about what they could not possibly reassure her about. She just looked down at, and played with, the sand like a little girl, because she had no power for anything else, certainly not for talk. She was having a tough time holding herself together, not just breaking down into tears, but something about the patience and easy solemnity of the fishermen calmed her just enough. The fishermen stood together in a group and talked, their voices raised because of the wind and the noise of the tumbling water. She could see them shaking their heads and kicking the sand and once in a while glancing over at her.

This continued for another twenty minutes, and then the fishermen seemed to have decided to hike down the bar toward the truck. Something had changed. One of them held a pair of field glasses. Leola pulled herself up and joined them, and in fact, she took hold of the arms of Billy and Wilson and stumbled along between them. They walked as close to the truck as they could, still fifty-some feet away, but now the whole crown of the cab was showing and a triangle of the cab window. So close, the water curling in the bed of the truck made a drumming sound.

It looked for a moment like a rock with seaweed tumbling about it, when Ron Diggs, who had the field glasses, said, "Well, shit," and Leola understood she was looking at the back of Hank's head in the water. Billy and Wilson both grabbed her and

Diggs handed her the glasses, and she saw it plain, then, the truth right there in the lenses, Hank's head bobbing, the hair rising and falling as if he were still driving, the window open on a summer day and he was just driving jauntily along as he always had, hillbilly music blasting away. The men held her back when Leola started forward, and she realized it was quite senseless to think she could go and open the door and let Hank out and give him a piece of her mind about last night, and then she felt hollow and was glad the men were holding her because otherwise surely she would just blow away, like a sheet of paper, a patch of fog.

Later, everyone was in her house, her mother and Hank's father, who kept asking for "what's his name again?" and neighbors and Hank's fishing pals, too. They had brought food. Even goddamn fish. So much fish. What was she supposed to do? I'm even short of chairs! she thought. Where are they all going to sit?

She slipped into the bedroom and shut the door and lay down, awash. She could hear people talking in the kitchen, the door opening and closing, even occasional laughter. She felt so far from everyone, just lying there feeling so ridiculous, embarrassed that she and Hank had ever made any plans, all of which were so suddenly obsoleted. It was like having an arm or a leg cut off, she thought, and you could still feel it. She heard Hank's father declaiming, "Well, what kind of restaurant is this?" and that jarred loose a memory of a night Hank and she had talked about Hank's father and the miserable progress of his disease, how erratic it was, and how infuriating and saddening it was to care for him. But neither Hank nor Leola could stand the idea of a nursing home. They would endure Hank's father and his troubles because, after all, look what the old man was enduring. Hank was drinking too many beers and Leola too much wine, unusual for both of them, and the more they drank, the more maudlin and goofy they became, at once seized by the pathos of

Hank's father's situation and the realization that the same could happen to them, and yet seized also by a terrible sense of absurdity and outright grotesquerie. Like the sight of the truck in the rip, Leola thought, absurd, grotesque, even funny if Hank had not been in it. Because? Because then it would have been just another story, a table-thumper, biggest catch of bass in Warrens' Bay history and old Hank dumps his truck off Good Rip, loses five hundred pounds!

"Honey," Hank had said, "when I get too old and too far gone, I just want you to put me in a rowboat and shove me off on the outgoing. Or pay somebody to tow me to the Gulf Stream."

"With a fishing rod, of course," Leola had said, a little sarcastically.

"Hell, yes. I'll troll if I can't cast," Hank had said. "I don't scorn drift fishin' neither."

"You'll probably meet a bunch of others out there," Leola said.

Hank laughed. "Wouldn't surprise me. Bunch of old farts, rowboats clustered around some ledges, dragging bait, waitin' to catch somethin' or die, whichever comes first."

"You know what they'll say?" Leola asked.

"Of course I know," Hank said, and together they started laughing, and then they really got a laugh going, not saying it, but each knowing very well what the other was thinking about what the old-timers in their death boats would say to Hank when he drifted up: *Brother, you shoulda been here yesterday!*

Someone knocked softly on the bedroom door.

"Go away," Leola said.

"Just checkin', Darlin'," Leola's mother said.

Go away, all of you, Leola thought. *At least keep them goddamn sandy wader boots off the rungs of my chairs!*

Lawson Fusao Inada

You know, I haven't changed all that much since October 1944. That was the Amache Concentration Camp, Colorado, U.S.A., and, of course, I still have the same family number: #29170. My uncle Tom, though, has since passed away—he was on furlough, with special permission to enter, visit, and bring a camera. He was also permitted to leave.

Lawson Fusao Inada is the author of *Before the War* (poems, Morrow, 1971), *Legends from Camp* (poems, Coffee House Press, 1992), and an editor of *AIIIEEEEE!* (Penguin, 1991) and *The Big AIIIEEEEE!* (New American Library, 1991). He is a professor of English at Southern Oregon State College.

Inada lives in Ashland, Oregon, "but is always from Fresno and the camps."

LAWSON FUSAO INADA
The Flower Girls

For children everywhere

I. The Meeting

*T*his is the story of Cherry and Rose, the two little girls who were almost sisters. They were almost twins, actually, because although they came from different families, they were both born on the very same day in the very same city of Portland, Oregon.

They met in the first grade on the very first day of school. They sat in the front row, right next to each other. They both had on pink dresses and white shoes. They even had their hair combed the same way—parted right down the middle. When the teacher saw them, she said, "Well, well, well—so you're Cherry, and you're Rose. Looks like we have a couple of real flower blossoms here. Why, I'll just call you my Flower Girls—and you can help me right now by passing out these pencils to the class. Come on, Flower Girls—let's go!"

Naturally, Cherry and Rose became best friends. From the very first day, they did everything together. They did very well in school, they ate lunch together, and during recess they jumped rope, played jacks, and played hopscotch together. They were good at things by themselves, but together they were even better.

II. After School

Now in those days, everyone walked home after school. The kids all lived close to school, but they went in different directions. Cherry went one way, and Rose went another. But one day, when school was over, Cherry said to Rose, "Rose, why don't you ask your mother if you could come over to my house to play tomorrow? I live just down over there and around the corner. We could have lots of fun, and I'll walk you home for dinner. Okay?"

"Okay!" said Rose.

So the next day, Rose went home with Cherry. As they got close, Cherry said, "I bet you can't guess where I live."

Rose said, "Over there?"

Cherry said, "No, silly—that's a newspaper office. Guess again."

Rose said, "Over there?'

Cherry said, "No, silly—that's the fish store. Guess again."

Rose said, "Over there?"

Cherry said, "No, silly—that's the manju-ya. You only get one more guess."

Then Rose said, "Well, how about that place?"

"Right," said Cherry.

"But what does that sign say?" said Rose.

"Don't be silly," said Cherry. "That sign says 'Sakura Tofu Company.'"

"But what does that mean?" said Rose.

"Don't be silly," said Cherry. "That means 'Cherry Blossom Tofu Company.'"

"But what is a tofu?" said Rose.

"Don't be silly," said Cherry. "A tofu is a tofu, don't you know?"

"But where do you live?" said Rose.

"Don't be silly," said Cherry. "We live in back of the store. Come on! My mom is waiting!"

Sure enough, Cherry's mom was waiting for them. A little bell tinkled when they went into the store. Cherry's mom said, "My, oh my—don't you Flower Girls look pretty today! Cherry, here's ten cents for you and Rose to spend. Why don't you show your friend around?"

"Okay!" said Cherry. "Let's go!"

III. Snow Cones and Manju

The girls had a great time that afternoon. It was a nice, warm day, and they walked around the busy neighborhood, looking in stores and saying hello to people. After a while, Rose said, "Cherry, what are we going to do with the ten cents?"

Cherry said, "Come on—I'll show you!"

They went into the place called the manju-ya. There were many good things to eat on the shelves—everything looked so pretty and colorful, and everything smelled so good and tasty. Rose said, "Boy, oh boy—I've never seen anything like this! What are we going to get?"

Cherry said, "I'll show you."

When the man came out from the back, Cherry said, "We'll have two snow cones, please—with rainbow flavors."

The man went over to the snow-cone machine, put in a big, shiny piece of ice, and cranked the ice around and around. He made snow, scooped the snow into paper cones, and poured all the flavors of the rainbow on top of the snow. The girls watched with wide-open eyes, and licked their lips.

Cherry gave the man ten cents, and they got their cones. Then the man said, "Just a minute." He got a small paper bag and put in some of the prettiest manju for them to take home, for free.

Naturally, the girls said, "Thank you, very much!"

They had to eat the snow cones pretty fast because it was a hot day, but if they ate too fast, it hurt their heads. So they walked down the sidewalk very slowly, being careful to eat with good manners, to not slurp too much, and to not spill anything on their dresses. Rose bumped into an old lady coming out of the fish store, but since nothing was spilled, they all laughed.

At the street corner, though, as they were finishing their snow cones, tipping the cones upside-down, Rose looked at Cherry and started to laugh.

"What's the matter?" said Cherry.

"You should look at your mouth!" said Rose.

"You should look at *your* mouth!" said Cherry.

And both girls went and looked into a mirror in the window of the beauty shop. They laughed when they saw their colorful mouths. They laughed some more when they saw some old ladies inside with curlers on their heads. The old ladies were laughing at them.

On the way to Rose's house, they stopped in the park and sat on a bench. Rose said, "I hope that snow cone won't spoil my supper. Now why don't we try some of that stuff in the bag?"

Cherry said, "Sure." They shared bits of one that was very soft and white, with something sweet and red inside. Cherry said, "Why don't you take the rest home to your mother?"

"Okay!" said Rose.

IV. Shaving the Ice

Rose had a lot to tell her mother that night about her best friend's neighborhood, and, before long, Rose was visiting Cherry almost every day after school. They played in Rose's neighborhood, too, doing what they called the "regular things"— like going to the grocery store, going to the butcher shop, and walking by the noisy factory full of big machines and boxes— but they both agreed that Cherry's neighborhood was much more interesting, so they played there most of the time.

At school, their teacher said, "My, oh my—you Flower Girls are almost like a secret club, always talking about things like 'manju' and 'tofu.' Can you girls explain some of that to me and the class?"

Rose said, "Manju is manju and tofu is tofu, but eating a snow cone is like eating Mount Hood!" Everybody laughed. Then Rose said, "And after eating a snow cone, you look like a clown because your mouth is all orange and purple and red!" Everybody laughed. Everybody wanted to try eating a snow cone.

Then the teacher said, "Class, a snow cone is just shaved ice." That made the class laugh even more, because who ever heard of shaving the ice?

One boy put his hand up and said, "Teacher, my daddy shaves his face every morning, but I didn't know that the ice had to shave!" Everybody laughed again.

V. Learning Names

As the year went by, all the children learned to read and write and count at school. But the Flower Girls also learned how to count in Japanese, from Cherry's mother, and they could point to their fingers and say "ichi, ni, san, shi" just like that. Then Cherry's mother taught the Flower Girls how to write their names in Japanese. It took practice, over and over, because it was almost like drawing a picture, but when they learned how to do it right, their names looked very fancy, very beautiful, and the Flower Girls felt very special when they showed the kids at school. The other kids tried to write their names in Japanese, too, and made a lot of funny marks on paper. The teacher couldn't write her name, either.

Cherry's mother was like a teacher at home, but a fun teacher, and she would explain things to the girls as they went with her to make deliveries. They would walk down the sidewalks carrying packages of tofu, and when Cherry's mother got paid, the girls would also say, "Arigato." That always made the customers smile.

Sometimes, the girls would play with dolls in the kitchen in back of the tofu store, and Cherry's mother would teach them interesting things like how to make cinnamon toast without burning the toast or spilling the cinnamon, or how to blow soap bubbles without making too much of a mess, or how to make glue and clean up afterwards, or how to answer the phone even though your mouth is full of peanut butter, or how to fold and cut newspapers into snowflakes and birds.

One day, Cherry's mother told the girls that Japanese names had very interesting meanings in Japanese, like "Ricefield" and "Pine Forest" and "Mountain River" and "Rocky Seashore." She said that everybody's name means something, and that names like "Portland" and "Multnomah" and "Oregon" mean something, too. And the same for "Columbia" and "Willamette" and "Roosevelt" and "Studebaker" and "Chevrolet" and "Ford."

"How about 'Burnside'?" asked Rose.

"Yes," said Cherry's mother, "that must mean something, too."

"How about 'Atkinson School'?" said Cherry.

"Yes, that must mean something, too," said Cherry's mother. "And the same for 'Atlantic' and 'Pacific' and 'Blitz Weinhard' and 'Jantzen Beach' and 'Washington Park' and 'Meier and Frank.' "

"How about 'Nabisco'?" said Cherry.

"Yes," said Cherry's mother, "that just means National Biscuit Company. Na-Bis-Co—you get it?"

"Sure we do!" said the Flower Girls.

VI. More Places and Names

Actually, Cherry's neighborhood had so many people, places, and names that the girls couldn't remember everything. There were places upstairs, there were places downstairs; there were places in front, there were places out back. There were barbershops, beauty shops, bathhouses, laundries, fish markets, dry goods stores ("What's dry goods?" asked the girls), grocery stores, stores full of appliances, shoe repair shops, auto repair shops, many restaurants, very many hotels, one newspaper office called the *Oh Shu*, one newspaper office called the *Nippo*, another newspaper office called the *Ka Shu*, doctors' offices, dentists' offices, and pharmacies ("What's a pharmacy?" asked the girls).

Sometimes, the Flower Girls would just walk around, saying names like songs. "*Oh Shu* and *Nippo* and *Ka Shu*—step right up and get your latest news!" At other times, they would play a game to see if they remembered all the churches. Portland Buddhist Church—that was easy. It was also called Bu-kyo-kai. Then there was Japanese Methodist Church—that was easy. But how about Ken-jyo-ji, Kon-ko-kyu, Minori-nakai, Nichiren, and Sei-cho—those were not as easy. So the girls would have to count them all on their fingers, like a test, and they would always pass.

One time, Cherry's mother said, "Girls, listen to the names of these clubs: Fukuoka-kenjinkai, Hiroshima-kenjinkai, Okayama-kenjinkai, Wakayama-kenjinkai, and Nippon-kenjinkai. Do you think you can remember all that?"

And the girls said, "Sure! We'll try! Say those again! You can't trick us!"

And Cherry's mother said, "Well, go-men-na-sai, Flower Girls!"

VII. The Dog Named Cat

One day, when Rose got home, she told her mother, "Mother, did you know that Cherry has a new puppy? It's brown and very soft and furry, but guess what she named it?" Her mother couldn't guess, so Rose said, "Cherry wanted a kitten instead, but since she's allergic to cats, she named her puppy Nekko. And Nekko means 'cat.' Do you get it, huh? Do you get it? Isn't that funny? Don't you think that's funny? She has a dog and a cat at the same time!" And then, after a while, Rose said, "Mother, can I get a dog or a cat?"

Another day, Rose came home and said, "Mother, did you

know that I was a hakujin? That's just what I am. And Cherry is a nihonjin. That's what she is. That's all. But we're both Americans. Isn't that interesting? And Cherry's mother says that we're *both* her Flower Girls."

Another time, Rose said, "Mother, did you know that where Cherry lives is called Shi-ta Machi? That means 'bottom town' or under or below. Isn't that interesting? Cherry's mother says that's because they live down by the river."

VIII. The Creature in the River

The teacher read a story to the class about the man in the moon. After it was over, Cherry raised her hand and told the class, "My mother says there is not a man in the moon but instead there are two rabbits with their hammers pounding rice." Some kids said that wasn't true, but Cherry said that when the moon was full they should go outside and *see* those rabbits that her mother showed her.

Cherry also said, "My mother says that the kappa is a creature who lives in the Willamette River. When you go down by the river, you can see his tracks. The kappa lives in the river, swimming under the boats and bridges, but he walks around on land at night. He likes to dump over garbage cans and play tricks on people."

One boy asked if the kappa likes to hurt people. Cherry said, "No, because he likes kids, but not even the police can catch him."

Another boy asked Cherry if she had seen the kappa.

Cherry said, "No, because I can't stay up at night. But one time I heard him. And in the morning, the garbage can was turned over."

One boy said that he had seen the kappa late at night, and that the kappa was big and hairy like a monster. Cherry said, "No, that's not the kappa, because the kappa is small, like a first-grader. Besides, he has a shell, like a turtle."

One girl asked if the kappa wore any clothes.

Cherry said, "No." Everybody laughed. Then Cherry said, "But you have to look out, because the kappa is very strong."

Then one boy said, "If the kappa ever came to my house, me and my dad would beat him up, just like that!"

Another boy said, "I would shoot him with a gun! Boom!"

And Cherry said, "Nobody could ever shoot or catch the kappa, because he's too fast. He could jump right into the river and swim right back to Japan. Or, if he wanted to, he could put on some clothes and walk around in a disguise, like a man."

One girl raised her hand and asked, "But why does he tip over garbage cans? Does he eat garbage?"

Cherry said, "No, he just does that, for fun."

One boy said, "But if he wears a disguise, how does he hide his face?"

Cherry said, "He wears a big, black hat. Besides, he could change his face to look like a man. And he wears a big overcoat to cover his shell."

Rose said, "One time, me and Cherry found a big overcoat in the alley. We didn't touch it. We ran home! The next day, it was gone!"

Everybody was quiet.

IX. The Celebrations

One day, after New Year's, Cherry told Rose that there was going to be a Girl's Day celebration in Shi-ta Machi, and that there would be many beautiful dolls on display, but not to play with. Then there was also going to be a Boy's Day when everybody would go on a picnic to a place called Montevilla, out in the country, to fly kites and play games, and that Rose could come with them. Then Cherry said that they could both dance in the Cherry Blossom Festival, too, but they would have to practice dancing after school.

"Oh, that will be fun," said Rose.

"Yes," said Cherry, "and we also get to wear special clothes."

Rose couldn't wait to get home to tell her mother. On the way home, she sang her own cherry blossom song. "Sakura, sakura," she sang, as she skipped along. "Sakura, sakura..."

The Flower Girls had a lot of fun at those special celebrations, and everybody said, "My, you Flower Girls are so beautiful!"

And one day, in the summer, Rose came home and told her mother, "Mother—guess what! Our teacher says we get to be in the Rose Parade! Isn't that great? We get to ride on a float! And Cherry says she's going to ride on the Shi-ta Machi float! Her float is going to have roses, too, but it is also going to have lots of fruits and vegetables on it, like strawberries and radishes and onions! Oh, I can't wait! Won't that be neat?"

X. In the Second Grade

So the Flower Girls rode in the Rose Parade, and they had a lot of fun playing together all that summer. Then, when school started again, they were both in the same class in the second grade, and they even sat in the same front seats, right next to each other. On the first day, the new teacher said, "Well, well, well—looks like we have the Flower Girls together again. Now, Flower Girls, will you help me pass out these brand-new books?"

School was so much fun, as usual, but one day, after Thanksgiving, when the class was going to start practicing on a Christmas play about Santa Claus and all the good little children, the teacher said, "Class, as you all know, America is having a war against Japan. But let's be good boys and girls and put on the best Christmas play we can. Okay?"

And all the kids said, "Okay!"

But that day, at recess, there were fights among the older kids in the playground, and a lot of kids got called "Jap!" Then a sixth-grade girl came up to Rose and Cherry and said, "You guys aren't supposed to play together because *she's* a *Jap* and *you're enemies!*"

And Rose said, "No we're not! *We're friends!*"

And the older girl said, "No you're not! You're enemies! You're having a war! Ha, ha, ha—you're having a war-ar! You're having a war-ar! Boo hoo hoo! Enemies, enemies, enemies! Ha, ha, ha—you're having a war-ar!"

XI. Just Because

The Christmas play was canceled, and it was not a very happy Christmas for anybody. The Flower Girls did not visit each other anymore, and one day, after New Year's, Cherry said to Rose, "We're not going to have a Girl's Day or a Boy's Day or a Cherry Blossom Festival this year."

And Rose said, "Why not? How come?"

And Cherry said, "Just because. Because we're having a war."

Then, on a fine, spring morning, the teacher said, "Class, as you know, some of you kids are going to be moving away soon, so this week let's all have a real nice good-bye party, okay?"

Nobody knew what to say.

At recess, Rose said, "Cherry, where are you going?"

Cherry said, "I don't know."

Rose said, "What do you mean you don't know? How come you don't know?"

"Because I don't know, stupid!" said Cherry. "All I know is that we're going down the river."

"But how come you're going down the river?" said Rose.

"Because we're going down the river, stupid!" said Cherry. "Because we're going to war."

"But how come you're going to war?" said Rose.

"Because we're Japs, stupid!" said Cherry.

"But how are you going?" said Rose. "I know—maybe you get to float on a boat! Maybe you get to float on a float!"

"Don't be stupid, stupid!" said Cherry. "I bet you wouldn't want to go."

"Yes, I would!" said Rose.

"That's because you're stupid, stupid!" said Cherry.

"I'm not stupid!" said Rose.

"Yes you are!" said Cherry. "You're stupid, stupid, stupid!"

The next day, Cherry said to Rose, "Rose, my mother wants to know if you could take care of Nekko for us."

"Why?" said Rose.

"Because we can't take her with us, stupid!" said Cherry.

"Why not? How come?" said Rose.

"Just because!" said Cherry. "Just because!"

XII. The Letters

On a warm, beautiful summer day, the mailman brought a letter to Rose. The letter said:

> Dear Rose,
> How are you? I am fine. How is Nekko? This
> place stinks. P U GARBAGE. Are you my
> friend? I can see Portland.
> > Your friend,
> > Cherry

With the help of her mother, Rose wrote a letter back to Cherry. The letter said:

> Dear Cherry,
> How are you? I am fine. Nekko got ran over.
> She went to heaven. I am your friend. You are
> in the map of Portland.
> > Your friend,
> > Rose

XIII. More Letters

On a lovely fall day, with a warm wind blowing, Cherry sat up in a bed and wrote a letter. The letter said:

> Dear Rose,
> How are you? I am fine. I am in the third

grade. Who is your teacher? My teacher is
American. We live in Idaho. I went to the
hospital. This is my picture of you and Nekko.
She is eating a manju. You are eating a snow
cone. This is my picture of you in the Rose
Parade. The float is beautiful. You are my
friend.

Your friend,
Cherry

The letter was never answered.

XIV. No One Knows

No one knows what happened to Cherry. No one knows
what happened to Rose. Shi-ta Machi is no more. The buildings
are still there, with different stores and businesses in them, but
the Shi-ta Machi people did not return to Shi-ta Machi. Shi-ta
Machi is no more.

There are still Shi-ta Machi people, though, living in all parts
of the city, and if you want to see Shi-ta, you have to look deep
into the eyes of the Shi-ta Machi people. You have to look deep
into the eyes, under the surface; you have to look deep below
the surface of the shining eyes. You have to look deep down to
the bottom of the eyes of the Shi-ta Machi people, and you will
see Shi-ta Machi shining in their eyes. You will see the shining
streets, the sidewalks full of people. You will see children like
Cherry and Rose, playing after school.

You will see the tofu store, you will see the manju-ya (you can
even smell the sweet manju, you can even hear the manju-man
shaving the ice, you can even taste the snow cone, oh, so cold,
with all the flavors of the rainbow). You can walk down the
sidewalks past all the stores and offices, and when you stop at the
corner, you can look into the window of the beauty shop and
see your face in the mirror.

Then, in the blink of an eye, Shi-ta Machi will be gone. Shi-
ta Machi is no more.

XV. The Song of Cherry and Rose

There is a beautiful park in the hills of Portland. It is full of trees and lawns, with many places to sit and play and walk and run. In one part of the park is a Japanese garden, full of beautiful plants and rocks, with a beautiful pond. In the Japanese garden, a very special cherry tree grows.

In the same part of the park, there is a beautiful rose garden. There are roses with all the colors of the rainbow, and in that garden grows a very special rose.

When the park is quiet, you can walk through the Japanese garden, and you can hear the wind blow. When the park is quiet, you can walk through the rose garden, and you can hear the wind blow.

The song you hear is the song of Cherry and Rose.

It is a beautiful song of friendship, of being best friends together, of going to school together, of playing together, of growing up together. It is a beautiful song of being the Flower Girls, of being sisters. It is a beautiful song of becoming women together, of always being sisters.

The song you hear is the song of Cherry and Rose.

XVI. The Continuing Story

On a fine, summer day, a family was on a picnic in the park. After lunch, the little girl said, "Mother, I'm going for a little walk through the rose garden. Okay?"

The little girl went walking through all the beautiful roses. Everything smelled like roses, felt like roses, everything was colored like roses. When the little girl was right in the middle of the rose garden, right when she was sniffing a big, red rose, she looked up and saw another little girl doing the same thing.

Both girls said "Hi!" at the same time. One girl said, "My name is Cherry. What's your name?"

The other girl said, "My name is Rose."

And Cherry said, "Do you want to walk over to the Japanese garden?"

And Rose said, "Okay. I'll ask my mother."

And Cherry said, "Okay. I'll ask my mother."

And Rose said, "Okay. I'll meet you back here. Okay?"

And Cherry said, "Okay. I'll meet you back here."

And off they went.

Acknowledgements

This story was made possible by a grant from the Metropolitan Arts Commission, Portland, Oregon.

Special thanks to: Terry Akwai, Keiko Archer, George Azumano, Kay Capron, Phin Capron, Chisao Hata, Corky Kawasaki, Kaz Kinoshita, Dr. and Mrs. Matt Masuoka, Peggy Nagae, Joan and Vern Rutsala, Lury Sato, Chiyo Shiogi, Woodrow Shiogi, Chiyoko Tateishi, Dr. James Tsujimura, Dr. and Mrs. Homer Yasui.

WESTERN DEFENSE COMMAND AND FOURTH ARMY
WARTIME CIVIL CONTROL ADMINISTRATION
Presidio of San Francisco, California

INSTRUCTIONS
TO ALL PERSONS OF
JAPANESE
ANCESTRY
LIVING IN THE FOLLOWING AREA:

All of that portion of the County of Multnomah, State of Oregon, bounded on the north by the Oregon-Washington State line, bounded on the east by 122nd Avenue, and 122nd Avenue extended southerly to the Multnomah-Clackamas County line, bounded on the south by the Multnomah-Clackamas County line, and bounded on the west by the Willamette River.

Pursuant to the provisions of Civilian Exclusion Order No. 26, this Headquarters, dated April 28, 1942, all persons of Japanese ancestry, both alien and non-alien, will be evacuated from the above area by 12 o'clock noon, P.W.T., Tuesday, May 5, 1942.

No Japanese person living in the above area will be permitted to change residence after 12 o'clock noon, P.W.T., Tuesday, April 28, 1942, without obtaining special permission from the representative of the Commanding General, Northwestern Sector, at the Civil Control Station located at:

> The Navy Post,
> American Legion Hall,
> 128 Northeast Russell Street,
> Portland, Oregon.

Such permits will only be granted for the purpose of uniting members of a family, or in cases of grave emergency.

The Civil Control Station is equipped to assist the Japanese population affected by this evacuation in the following ways:

1. Give advice and instructions on the evacuation.

2. Provide services with respect to the management, leasing, sale, storage or other disposition of most kinds of property, such as real estate, business and professional equipment, household goods, boats, automobiles and livestock.

3. Provide temporary residence elsewhere for all Japanese in family groups.

4. Transport persons and a limited amount of clothing and equipment to their new residence.

THE FOLLOWING INSTRUCTIONS MUST BE OBSERVED:

1. A responsible member of each family, preferably the head of the family, or the person in whose name most of the property is held, and each individual living alone, will report to the Civil Control Station to receive further instructions. This must be done between 8:00 A. M. and 5:00 P. M. on Wednesday, April 29, 1942, or between 8:00 A. M. and 5:00 P. M. on Thursday, April 30, 1942.

2. Evacuees must carry with them on departure for the Assembly Center, the following property:

    (a) Bedding and linens (no mattress) for each member of the family;

    (b) Toilet articles for each member of the family;

    (c) Extra clothing for each member of the family;

    (d) Sufficient knives, forks, spoons, plates, bowls and cups for each member of the family;

    (e) Essential personal effects for each member of the family.

All items carried will be securely packaged, tied and plainly marked with the name of the owner and numbered in accordance with instructions obtained at the Civil Control Station. The size and number of packages is limited to that which can be carried by the individual or family group.

3. No pets of any kind will be permitted.

4. No personal items and no household goods will be shipped to the Assembly Center.

5. The United States Government through its agencies will provide for the storage at the sole risk of the owner of the more substantial household items, such as iceboxes, washing machines, pianos and other heavy furniture. Cooking utensils and other small items will be accepted for storage if crated, packed and plainly marked with the name and address of the owner. Only one name and address will be used by a given family.

6. Each family, and individual living alone, will be furnished transportation to the Assembly Center or will be authorized to travel by private automobile in a supervised group. All instructions pertaining to the movement will be obtained at the Civil Control Station.

Go to the Civil Control Station between the hours of 8:00 A. M. and 5:00 P. M., Wednesday, April 29, 1942, or between the hours of 8:00 A. M. and 5:00 P. M., Thursday, April 30, 1942, to receive further instructions.

J. L. DeWitt
Lieutenant General, U. S. Army
Commanding

April 28, 1942

See Civilian Exclusion Order No. 26.

Lee Martin

This picture was taken when I was in the fourth grade—the year I fell in love with Patty Duke, the year my teacher told me I had no imagination.

Lee Martin is a doctoral student at the University of Nebraska at Lincoln. He received his M.F.A. in 1984 from the University of Arkansas.

Martin's stories have appeared in such places as *Indiana Review*, *Yankee*, *Other Voices*, and *Sonora Review*. He has new work forthcoming in *Story* and *New England Review*.

LEE MARTIN
Secrets

*E*ach half hour, Oren goes outside and shines his flashlight on the thermometer tacked to the front of the house. He leaves the door open, and Glenna, dishes done, smells rain, hopes it will be gentle when it comes—a steady, soaking rain to last the night.

She knows he is not checking the temperature, that the thermometer is only an excuse, that what he is really doing is listening for the dogs: Moad Keen's hounds, no respecters of crops and gardens, set loose three nights this week chasing fox.

"If they come through here tonight," Oren has promised, "I'll be ready." His rifle, a Remington .30–.30, is leaning against his recliner. His crossword puzzle books are on the table, his reading glasses, his Valium.

She knows he is all bluster and bluff: the way his hands tremble, he could never hold a rifle's bead. She wishes he would forget the dogs, wishes they would get in the car and go visiting like they did when they were younger. She recalls summer nights, late August, the wheat harvested, the soybeans and corn filling pod and husk, when he would drive her to the Bethlehem store for ice cream: vanilla or strawberry-swirl. How they would sit outside on the old Church of Christ pews, the women in their summer dresses, the men in clean overalls and caps, talking softly in the dark, chores done, and old Delbar Tapley rising, fiddle tuned, rosin gleaming on the cocked bow.

Who knew then that Oren would get Parkinson's disease, would take Valium, but only half a tab for fear he might become an addict, just enough to help him sleep. And Glenna would sleep alone in a room across the hall, hear him at night shifting about in his bed until he gave up and shuffled to the living room to sit in lamplight working crossword puzzles or reading Carl Sandburg's biography of Lincoln—a good, true book, he has told her, about a decent man.

Tonight, he wears pajamas as yellow as lemon ice cream. "Rain coming." He shuts the door. "If it drops below seventy, I'll cut the AC and open up the house."

"Leave it," she says. "Mercy. Don't let it trouble your soul."

They watch a program on television, a western, but not like the old "Gunsmoke" show. This one has robots in it: bionic gunslingers. They look so much like regular men, no one can tell they are indestructible, all circuits and wires. They keep terrorizing the town. No one, not even the brave sheriff, can stop them.

Oren says, well of course, that is all nonsense. "Just a made-up story," he says. "Not a word of it true."

Halfway through the program, their granddaughter Tess stops by with a box of Grandma Harp's Depression glass. "I want you to keep this for me," she says.

She is tall and slim-hipped with veins that kick and twitch in the papery skin around her eyes. She is wearing cowboy boots and tight Levi's, and a T-shirt cut off at her navel.

"You ought to put on some clothes," Oren says.

"Me?" Tess laughs. "You're the one in your pj's."

"Smart aleck," says Oren, and takes his flashlight outside.

Tess sets the box on the couch.

"I gave those dishes to you last Christmas," Glenna says.

"Granny, you know I won't have room for them in town."

"You'll have to make a place for them someday." Glenna squeezes her arm in what she hopes will pass for a playful gesture. "After we're both gone."

"Granny," says Tess, "how you talk."

Glenna has a frightening thought. "Promise me you'll never sell them, Tess."

"Why, Granny. Do you think I'd ever do that?"

Glenna would not be surprised, not one bit. Young ones . . . well, they are different, is all she can say. She remembers how she and her mother cared for Grandma Harp. How the old woman, bedfast, lay in the dark, curtains drawn, bed table littered with medicines: camphor and castor oil, Epsom salts and horehound. She called Glenna in each evening and asked her to sing hymns—"Blessed Assurance," "Bringing in the Sheaves," "Sweet Hour of Prayer"—and Glenna obliged, never once considered withholding her favor.

Now, as she examines the Depression glass, as she handles the thin saucers and plates, the pink glass etched with fleurs-de-lis, she remembers the name of the pattern is American Sweetheart. She imagines she will be the last of her family to know the name; even if she tells it to Tess, she fears she will forget it. She is certain Tess's mother, Joanne, does not remember, and she knows Joanne—who lives in Sweden and telephones twice a year: once on Christmas and once on Mother's Day—will never care for her or Oren when that time comes, nor will Tess.

At first this knowledge angers her, but as hard as she tries, she cannot muster an abiding malice. It is just the way it is done these days. The old ones are carted off to nursing homes. Their neighbor lady, Evangeline Harms, ended up there. Evangeline Harms, who taught school for thirty-eight years—who fastened galoshes, and bandaged cuts, and swabbed Mercurochrome on scraped knees. In the end it didn't matter. In the end, Glenna knows, nothing you have done or been will save you.

She sees, through the picture window, the beam of Oren's flashlight jerking over her flower beds—marigold and zinnia in all their glory.

"How is he?" Tess asks.

If she dared speak the truth, Glenna would admit his balance is going; twice this month he has fallen, and his hands shake so badly she has taken to signing all his checks. But truth, in this case, is too humbling a confession.

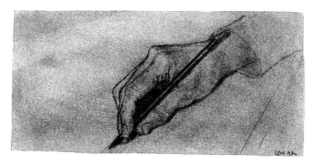

She can recall the exact moment she knew they were old. A day last fall, when Oren, picking apples, asked her to steady the stepladder. "Hold fast," he told her. At the top, he reached his skinny arm out into the air and she saw the pale flesh, loose on the muscle, chill and quiver. His hand shook as he groped for the apples, the Red Delicious, coddled them into the bushel basket resting on the ladder's top step. When he had finished, he stayed at the top, staring straight ahead. "What's wrong?" she asked.

"Just catching my breath," he said.

But she knew he was afraid to come down, afraid like a cat gone too far out on a limb, and what was more, she was afraid for him. "Just step down," she told him. "Leave the basket. I'll get it later. Take one step. I'm holding on."

They have these secrets, facts they harbor, hints of their demise. They do not tell them to Tess, not even to their friends. They speak of them infrequently to themselves.

"Your grandfather is fine," she says.

Oren comes inside, sweat beaded on his lip. "I hear those dogs." He lays the flashlight on the table. "Sounds like off in the bottoms."

"Moad Keen's hounds," Glenna says to Tess.

"Took out three tomato plants last night," says Oren. "Night before, they were into the sweet corn."

"You can't stop those dogs." Tess takes his arm and helps him down into his recliner. "They just run where they want." Oren picks up the rifle and lays it across his legs. "Granddad," she says, "quit acting the fool."

"Don't worry about me," he says. "You've problems enough of your own."

Tess and her husband Kenneth are losing their farm. The FmHA has foreclosed, and O.B. Ritchey, the auctioneer, has tagged equipment and livestock for sale. Tess and Kenneth are moving into town, into a double-wide trailer close to the garment factory where Tess is a seamstress. Kenneth, optimistic, as if some great load has left him, feels certain he can catch on with his cousin's building and remodeling business. He was never much of a farmer anyway, he says. Maybe it's all for the best.

Oren agrees. He could have given them money, enough to have kept them afloat, but that would have been a patch-up job, nothing that would have held. Better to let it go, he told Glenna, while they were young, with another chance, and time enough to take it.

What Oren does not know is that Tess has become involved with Spec Green, a DeKalb seed salesman, thinks she loves him—him with his eyeglasses, and his clean boots, and his big hands that smell of shelled corn. A secret she confessed to Glenna last spring on Decoration Day when they were setting coffee cans full of peonies on the family graves at the Gilead Cemetery.

"It's your business," Glenna told her.

"Oh, Granny. I feel so silly. Kenneth and I used to be locked together as tight as a dovetail joint. Now here I am, thirty-one years old, all loose at the hinges." She lifted her shoulders and let them drop. "I don't know a thing about love."

"Why, what a thing to say," said Glenna, unsettled by the fact that anyone dare question something so sacred. Wasn't the mystery the most of it? Still, it frightened her to think she herself had never before considered the carpentry of love. Had she missed something? She who had lived over seventy years. Had she not once, since the night she first met Oren at a Methodist camp meeting, called to measure the braces and joists of their hearts?

"Don't worry," she said. "I won't tell your grandfather." Mismanagement of a farm he could stomach, but barely. The immoral heart was, of course, another matter.

"Granny, you look after him," Tess whispers to her as she is leaving.

"You can't tell him anything," says Glenna. "Hardheaded. He'll do what he wants."

What he wants is sleep, but tonight, like most nights, it shies away. He tries all the old tricks—drinking warm milk, counting sheep, remembering happy moments from his life—but nothing works. He has left the Valium in the living room, a last resort he will fall back on toward dawn, if need be. The digital clock Tess and Kenneth gave him last Christmas counts off the minutes, the numbers going *cl-clack* each time a new one flips over.

He has kept the air conditioner on, at Glenna's insistence, even though he cannot abide its drone. He would gladly sacrifice comfort to be able to open a window and listen to the night: the hot breeze rustling cabbage leaves and cornstalks in the garden, hungry hogs banging at the feeder lids, an owl somewhere far off in the hollow.

And what of the dogs? Moad Keen's hounds? When Oren last heard them, he could tell they had turned and were running east, back up toward the high ground. He imagines them swimming the Little Wabash, thrashing on toward the timber along the ridges, claws scrabbling over shale, water dripping from muzzles and bellies, the fox always before them, and Moad Keen creeping along the gravel roads in his pickup, listening for their calls: the bitch's bay, the pup's bullfrog gump.

How is it, Oren wonders, that Moad shoulders his life. A man never married, living alone in what used to be Hadley School a mile off the Sumner blacktop. A man who breeds mystery, rooting for ginseng the way he does, running his trotlines, curing pelts. A man people tolerate but never befriend. The one they hope never comes calling to ask a favor, to borrow a wrench, to hire out for work. Any lie—*I've got all the hayhands I need, Moad*—so obvious a sign he does not belong.

Oren tries to imagine a life without Glenna. He remembers his brother Jim dying in a veterans' hospital in St. Joseph, Missouri. He lived alone in a trailer park off the beltway, pumped gas at a Shell station, and drank. That was what people knew about him. But Oren, when he came to claim the body, could have told them much more: how when they were boys Jim played harmonica, sang in the school Christmas pageant, received a certificate once for one hundred perfect spelling lessons. Those were the details he remembered, but he knew, even if he had had the nerve to speak, the doctors would not have been interested.

They wanted to perform an autopsy. The thought of Jim cut and gutted seemed indecent, but the doctors said they could learn something, something that could help others, so Oren signed the consent form, a secret he has always kept from his sister and other brother, something he still troubles over on nights like this when he cannot sleep. Was it the right thing? Does it matter now? He wonders if this is what naturally comes with age: a concern for decency, a fear of sin and offense.

And now these dogs set upon him like a curse. He would like to ignore them. Patience is a virtue, Glenna always says. But he has never been particularly Christian, not even now toward the end of his life.

A pain starts up his leg, an ache in his calf muscle. Too cool in the air conditioning, even beneath the sheet. He throws on a summer robe, sits on the edge of the bed, and fumbles in the dark for his house slippers.

In the kitchen, he drinks some water, leaning over the sink, his hand trembling. He uses a dish towel to wipe his chin.

He steps outside—a breath of air is what he needs. The wind is up, and between the rolls of thunder he hears the hounds yelping somewhere in his woods, to the south, somewhere beyond the tree line, the pack of them, noses to the scent. Some twenty rods away, he gauges. And coming fast.

In her bedroom, Glenna is dreaming about Arizona. She is nineteen, Oren is twenty-one. It is 1937, and they have driven here on their honeymoon in Oren's father's Buick. They have driven all day to see the Grand Canyon and have arrived late in the afternoon. Still, the sun is glaring on the red sandstone. Daylight, this far west, will stretch on yet for hours.

Oren is in his shirt-sleeves; Glenna is in a summer dress, so white in the sun it gleams. They have just shared the last Pepsi-Cola from an old metal cooler borrowed from Glenna's aunt, and the ice has melted, leaving a good three inches of water in the bottom.

"Watch this." Oren pours the water over the rim of the canyon, and they watch as it comes apart, separating into crystals that grow smaller and smaller, sparkling until they evaporate and disappear, not nearly halfway down.

She is dreaming all this when she hears the shot. At first she imagines the thunder has startled her. Then Oren is standing in the doorway, his shoulders slumped, the .30-.30 held in one hand, barrel down.

"Did you hear?" he asks.

"I heard."

A set of headlights sweeps over the wall, settling on Oren, whitewashing his face.

"I hit one. You didn't think I would." He leans the rifle against the wall. "It's done now, and I can't say I'm sorry."

The knock on the front door comes loud and explosive. They stare at each other, not speaking.

He wants to tell her he is afraid, not of Moad Keen whose hound lies dead in the barn lot, not of the Valium, not of the Parkinson's even, or of dying. No, it is something more than that, something more difficult to explain. A knowledge he has that these are their last days, that he does not believe in the soul, that what stops here—love, even its memory—stops. It is the loss of that, above all else, he mourns.

And Glenna is thinking she must remember to tell Tess that love, at long last, gives up its secret. Not in words she can pass along, only in a feeling as thin as a shiver, barely a whisper on a night she has been moving toward all her life: a night when she knows she has always been in the place she belongs. Patience, she will tell her. Stay with someone long enough. Stay until you are old.

She folds back the sheet and pats the mattress. Oren eases into bed beside her. They lie together, but do not touch, and while Moad Keen pounds on the door, neither knows that the other is recalling Arizona: how Oren poured water into the Grand Canyon, how it shattered like glass. They watched the last bits drizzle away until nothing was left—no proof, no sign. Enormous space below them, all that dry air.

"Like magic," Glenna said.

"No," said Oren. "It's more like something broke."

The rain comes. It falls in silver sheets. Falls over the fields and the river. Over the pup dead in the barn lot. Over Moad Keen who stands in the rain, whistling, shoulders pitched forward, waiting for someone to answer.

We have no photo available.

Sigrid Nunez

Sigrid Nunez has published stories in *The Threepenny Review*, *The Iowa Review*, *Glimmer Train Stories*, *Salmagundi*, and other journals. She has been the recipient of two Pushcart Prizes and of a G.E. Foundation Award for Younger Writers. A reading of one of her stories was broadcast recently by KPFA in San Francisco.

Nunez lives in New York City.

Sigrid Nunez (signature)

SIGRID NUNEZ

The Loneliest Feeling in the World

*I*t was Memorial Day. Sally Miller was taking her twin sons to their grandparents' farm, where they were to spend their summer vacation. They had driven about half the way when she saw the man standing smack in the middle of the road. His knees were so bent, he looked as if he were sitting on the edge of an invisible chair.

"Look: a drunk," said a voice from the back seat—Sally was not sure whose. To her eyes the twins' faces were as different as those of any two children, and it always surprised her when others—even their grandparents and occasionally their own father—confused them. But their voices were utterly indistinguishable; everyone agreed about that.

Drunk? It was morning yet. They were miles from any town, and there was not another car in sight. How came a drunk to be staggering way out here?

"Dad says don't stop," Toby reminded his mother, hanging his chin over the front seat.

"Yeah," said Tod. "You never know. He could be some kind of weirdo, a killer or something."

The boys were right; her husband was right: you never did know. But Sally, who at the age of ten had used her roller skate to beat off a dog that had attacked a schoolmate, was not going

Glimmer Train Stories, Issue 5, Winter 1993
©1992 Sigrid Nunez

to let fear stop her from helping someone who might be hurt. She slowed the car—had to hit the brake hard as the man lurched right in their path. The twins knocked heads with a resounding crack but were too agog to complain.

Now that she had stopped, Sally felt a heave of anxiety. Remembering that all the doors were open, she reproached herself for not having at least taken the precaution of locking them.

Slowly, leaning his weight on his left hand, with which he groped along the side of the car, the man approached Sally's door. Fear tightened her throat, but when she spoke her voice was normal. "You got trouble?"

The man shook his head—but not in response to her question, Sally realized. He was in a daze, like someone just waking up. There was dark stubble on his cheeks, one of which bore an unusual scar: a round, brownish pink hollow that looked a lot like a navel. Smooth, close-shorn brown hair hugged his scalp like the pelt of a large field mouse. He was about forty, Sally guessed. His T-shirt and Levi's looked as if he had slept in them. But though his eyes were threaded with red, there was no trace of alcohol on his breath.

Without answering, the man peered through the windows of the car as though at never-before-seen forms of life in an aquarium. His jaw hanging loose, he looked pretty doltish; it occurred to Sally that he might be a moron. A twin started giggling. Sally waited. Finally the man spoke: "Ma'am, can you please tell me where I *am*?" He drew out the last word in a kind of moan, piteous to hear.

"About a hundred miles northwest of Milwaukee," Sally told him. "Did you have an accident or something? Are you hurt? Where's your car? Or were you hitching?"

After each question the man blinked, and after each blink his eyes opened wider in astonishment. "I don't have the faintest idea how I got here," he said. He gazed about vaguely at the acres

78   *Glimmer Train Stories*

of pastureland stretching along both sides of the road.

Alarmed, but wishing to hearten, Sally tried lightness: "Tied one on last night and your buddies left you for dead—something like that?"

The man wagged his head doubtfully. "I don't think I've been drinking." Sally didn't think so either. And if she was becoming more and more dismayed, it was not because she thought the man was dangerous but because he seemed so hopelessly lost.

"Well, where do you live?" she asked, still trying to sound bright. The man looked at her for a moment as though he hadn't understood, then assumed an expression Sally had seen once before—on the face of a man who couldn't swim and who'd accidentally stumbled into a pool. She named the nearest towns in either direction. The man chewed his lips and frowned. Sally could hardly bring herself to ask the next question: "What is your name?"

The man shrugged helplessly. Sally was incredulous. "No wallet, no ID?" He slapped his pants pockets, front and back: nothing.

"Amnesia!" cried Tod, in a tone of such unmistakable delight his mother cringed. "Someone musta conked you one. Does your head hurt?"

"Be quiet, Toby," Sally snapped. The man didn't answer. A few seconds passed during which no one spoke and the chirping of grasshoppers seemed very loud. A hawk wheeled in the clear blue space overhead.

"Get in," Sally said at last. "I'll take you to Schocken." For this seemed to her the most reasonable thing to do. "It's about ten miles down this road. Nice people. I broke down once just outside of town. I'll drive you to the sheriff's; he's right off the road."

The man hesitated, opened his mouth as though to speak, sighed instead, and walked slowly around to the other side of the car.

Quite a stir in the back as he slid into the seat beside Sally. The twins were amazed and overjoyed that their mother had done this forbidden thing: inviting a strange man into the car.

But Sally didn't think she was taking a risk. The man was no faker, she was certain of that. No question but that something terrible had happened to him, possibly something belonging to that order of bizarre tragic events—like the Swensens' perfectly healthy newborn's heart stopping one day for no reason at all—that shook your faith to its roots. As she started the car, she tried to imagine what it must be like, sitting there without a clue as to who you were or where you belonged, and she decided it must be the loneliest feeling in the world.

Lonely was not the first word the man would have used to describe how he felt at this moment. He was too busy trying to grasp what had happened. Among his first thoughts was the terrifying possibility that he had gone mad. He didn't feel mad, exactly; but, just as surely, he did not feel sane. He felt as if he had plunged from a towering height and were still falling. His limbs were light; his skin, cool. When the woman spoke, her voice seemed to come from on high. Did his head hurt? the boy wanted to know. Oh, it did. It hurt mightily—he had no idea why. Drink? Hunger? Accident? Fight? He massaged his scalp gingerly with the fingertips of one hand: no bump, no scab. The furthest back he could remember was just minutes before the woman in the car appeared. He had woken to find himself lying on his stomach in the manure-strewn pasture. With difficulty, he had gained his feet and headed for the road, knees buckling, rhinestones swirling before his eyes. He hadn't even seen the green Chevy coming.

As they drove along, the twins kept up a low buzz, murmuring into each other's ears and craning their necks to ogle his profile. And what they saw was a mystery to him, for when he tried to picture his own face, he saw only a brown and pink blur. Indeed, now that he tried, the man discovered that he could not summon a single familiar face to mind. Not one image of kith or kin.

He gazed forlornly at the knolly green landscape with its clusters of browsing Holsteins. Had you asked him what kind of country they were in, he could have told you: it was dairy country. If this old Chevy were to break down, he was pretty sure he could fix it. If he had to, he could take the wheel. The woman had mentioned Milwaukee, and that, he knew, was the biggest city in the state of Wisconsin, famous for bratwurst and beer. What he didn't know was whether he had ever been there. He had no idea where he had been, even so short a time ago as this morning. He was tired, his body ached, he needed a bath, and he could imagine perfectly what it would be like to sleep, to wash. Hunger he knew, and thirst, and fear. (Earlier, at the word *sheriff*, he had felt his pulse quicken and this scared him: might he be in trouble with the law?) He glanced quickly at the woman beside him. She was about thirty-five, not quite pretty but still girlish-looking, with her hair swept up in a fat ponytail. The two in the back would be her kids. He reckoned their age at about eight. They were what you called identical twins. But wasn't it damn peculiar? How was it possible for a man to know all these things and not his own name?

They had reached Schocken. Sally made a right and turned off the road. As they entered the town, she tried to think of something inspiriting to say to the stranger, so uneasily still at her side. Now they were already pulling up at the sheriff's. "Would you like me to go in with you?" she asked.

"Oh, no, you don't have to do that," said the man, getting out of the car. "You've done enough, thank you. You've done plenty, thank you so much."

Sally watched as he headed for the door of the squat brick building, taking short, halting steps, as if his shoes pinched. Then, with as much cheer as she could muster, she called after

him: "Don't worry. It'll all come back, you'll see." The man
turned and nodded uncertainly. Sally waited till he had gone
through the door before driving away.

An earsplitting hubbub erupted behind her. Now that the man
was gone, the twins speculated about his identity, transforming
the meek, troubled soul they had just dropped off into the villain
they were half hoping for when they picked him up. Listening
to them jabber about the mass murderer, escaped convict, or
space alien back at the sheriff's, Sally realized that they were
going to be talking about this little adventure for some time.
Then she forgot the stranger's worries and considered her own:
the next time the boys talked to their father they'd be full of
stories about the man with the belly button in his face, and, oh,
would she catch hell.

Sheriff Bitz was not in. He was out of town, celebrating the
holiday at a barbecue to which the Bitzes had been invited by the
parents of their daughter Annie's fiancé. The boy's father was
one of the biggest cheese makers in the state. The Big Cheese
himself was how Sheriff Bitz liked to refer to him. The future
in-laws would be meeting one another for the first time today,
and Sheriff Bitz could not hide the truth from his deputy: he was
as nervous as he was pleased.

Kurt Hollis understood. It was a big day for him, too, and he
was intensely nervous and intensely pleased. Today he had
Sheriff Bitz's permission to close the office early. There was just
a little paperwork that needed to be done that morning; then he
was free to meet Freya Lockhart who, to his joy and disbelief,
had agreed to accompany him to the Memorial Day stock car
races, at which his brother Roy was to compete. This, after an
entire year of alternately raised and dashed hopes. Kurt was just
about ready to leave the office, trembling with anticipation at the
thought of Freya's radiant blue eyes and perfectly heart-shaped
face, when the man walked through the door.

Kurt listened to the extraordinary story with his mouth half open. "Some kind of amnesia, huh?" was all he could think to say. Well, what was to be done? He supposed he ought to call Sheriff Bitz. But it didn't seem right, did it—bothering him on an important day like this? Might even irk him, Kurt worried, remembering that Bitz had asked not to be disturbed, except for a matter of life and death—which, of course, Kurt knew was only a manner of speaking, but still: shouldn't he be able to handle this sort of case by himself? He'd been deputy for a little over a year now. Wasn't it about time he learned how to take responsibility—he, a man of twenty-two, a man thinking of settling down with Freya Aurelia Lockhart?

Stalling for time, Kurt took up a pen and started scribbling on a blank report form. The man waited patiently on the other side of the desk, shifting his weight from foot to foot. Kurt wrote out a description of the man, as he would of a suspect. But, of course, the man wasn't a suspect . . . there was no suspect . . . no crime had been committed . . . but the man's wallet was missing . . . he might have been robbed . . . on the other hand, the man wasn't reporting a robbery . . . Oh dear, oh dear.

The telephone rang, and Kurt shivered at Freya's slow, thick voice, which always sounded, according to his mother, as though she'd just eaten a whole box of chocolate creams. (Mrs. Hollis had not meant this kindly.)

Would Kurt please stop and pick up some cigarettes on his way to Freya's house?

Of course he would, but—Kurt chewed his ballpoint, nodded awkwardly at the man, and briefly explained the matter to Freya.

"Well, he didn't just fall out of the sky, he's got to belong somewhere," said Freya. "Hasn't anyone reported a missing person?"

"Nope."

"So maybe he's from out of town. Call the state troopers."

"Okay, okay," Kurt agreed breathlessly, "but—" again he bit

his pen, this time with such force he felt a shooting pain in his jaw, "I just want you to know I may be held up here until this thing is taken care of." He smiled apologetically at the thing to be taken care of. "You'll wait, won't you, Freya?" There was a pause during which Kurt saw all his future happiness whisked away: a vision of Freya and a pair of indistinct children clustered before a deep-porched house flickered and vanished, like a scene glimpsed from a speeding train.

At last Freya said, "Well, I'll wait *some*." Then she added, more petulantly, "I guess I'll get the cigarettes myself." She hung up, and Kurt might have wept had he not noticed the man listing and wobbling like a scarecrow in a gale.

Oh dear, oh dear. What now? Was he ill?

"You okay there?" Kurt asked, hastening around the desk and cupping the man's elbow in his palm. The man shuddered slightly at Kurt's touch.

"Oh, just a little weak," he said, in a voice that was very weak indeed.

"You need a doctor, you think?"

"No, I—food, more likely. I don't know when I ate last but it feels like a while."

There was a diner a few doors up the street. It would take just five minutes for Kurt to run there and fetch something; meanwhile the man could rest on the cot in the cell in the adjoining room.

"But I got no money," the man protested when Kurt suggested this.

"No need to worry about that," Kurt said soothingly. "You just lie down now and rest." He guided the man through the door toward the cell, wishing there were a more respectable place to put him. The cell, which Kurt blushed to see was none too clean, did not get much use. Occasionally, Mr. Hefernan, whose tottery mental balance depended on medication, skipped a few doses and had to be kept away from the schoolyard; or one or another of the unruly regulars at the pool bar might be hauled in to cool off for a night. "What do you want to eat?"

"Oh—anything," said the man, lowering himself onto the cot. "Sandwich—anything."

"Rita's meat loaf is superior," Kurt hinted. The man nodded absently and Kurt hurried out.

The diner was crowded with early lunchers. Breathless from running, Kurt ordered the sandwich and a Coke from Rita, a burly woman with huge, rough-knuckled fists like a working-man's. He could not resist telling her whom the food was for.

"Isn't that something," Rita said, pouring Kurt a cup of coffee to drink while he waited for the sandwich to be made. "What's he look like?"

Kurt shrugged. "Nothing special. I'd say about forty, tallish, maybe six foot, maybe one-seventy, dark, plain features. Looks like any guy except for this funny scar on his cheek, kind of a dent, like someone poked him with something."

"And he can't even remember his own name?"

"Nope. Can't remember a damn thing about himself." Kurt was aware that several people at the counter had turned their attention to him, and he felt at once important and shy, in the manner of one who has lived all his life in the shadow of a dashing, more accomplished and popular brother.

The sandwich was ready. Kurt paid for it and trotted back to the office.

The man stood scrutinizing his reflection in the tarnished oval mirror that hung over the cell washbasin. He accepted the food with a mixture of thanks and embarrassment. Kurt, himself embarrassed, left the man immediately and returned to his desk.

Freya was right. He ought certainly to call the state troopers. But the sheriff had a rule: under no circumstances was Deputy Hollis to report any matter to the state police without first checking with him. ("Save us a ton of red tape and a red face, too," was how Bitz put it.) So, as much as he disliked the idea,

Kurt had no choice: he'd have to bother Bitz.

He was just about to pick up the phone when the front door opened and in popped a small brown rabbit of a woman, wringing her paws in obvious distress. To Kurt's immense relief she announced that her husband had been missing for two days. Without waiting to hear more, Kurt hustled the woman back to the cell, where the man sat on the edge of the cot, finishing his sandwich.

"Oh, Clayton, thank God!"

The man looked at his wife as though he had no idea who she was. Kurt was amazed, but the woman showed no hint of surprise. Turning to Kurt, she spoke in a hushed, apologetic tone (as if it were *her* fault, Kurt thought sympathetically): "It happens now and then. He gets so—confused, he can't remember things. Then he wanders off, gets lost. He'll be all right once I get him home." Kurt nodded understandingly, thinking of poor abashed Mrs. Hefernan, hanging her head on that very spot each time she came to collect her kinky husband.

The woman took a step nearer to the cot, returning her husband's bewildered gaze with one of affectionate concern. "Oh, Clayton," she sighed. "You had me so worried." Then she held out her hands to him. "Come: let's go home."

Without a word the man rose and followed his wife out of the cell as obediently as he had followed Kurt into it. The two were about to leave the office when Kurt said, "Wait a minute. Why don't you give me your name, so I know who to get in touch with, you know—" he paused, trying to think of a tactful way to put it, "in case you ever need us again."

Over her shoulder the woman said, "Emma McBroom. Acorn Lane," and went out, leading her husband by the hand.

Alone, Kurt threw back his head, pounded his chest, and let out a little hoot like the young ape that he was. The McBrooms had hardly gone when he stood outside the door, fumbling with his key. He felt enormously happy and pleased with himself, as though after a difficult business adroitly dispatched. But he knew he hadn't actually *done* anything—just been lucky.

As he finally managed to insert the key in the lock, a dirty joke from high school days came back to him. And though there was no one to see him, he blushed; though there was no one to hear, he laughed out loud, thinking: Well, maybe later today he'd be lucky in that, too.

Driving through the unfamiliar town in an old, unfamiliar dove-gray sedan, Clayton sat speechless beside his unfamiliar wife. Innumerable questions clamored in him, but he was in too great a state of shock to articulate them. He wondered how long he had been married and whether he had any children. He wondered how he had gotten that funny scar in the middle of his left cheek. Above all, he wondered when his memory would come back to him. Though he no longer felt faint, his head ached worse than ever, and his heart had not stopped pounding since he and Emma left the sheriff's office. Having to be prepared every minute to learn some new fact about yourself could sure put a man on tenterhooks. But there was this consolation: he was no longer all alone in the world. He had a name. He knew where he belonged. And there existed someone who could at least begin to answer his many questions.

He stole a peek at his wife, who kept glancing from the road to smile at him as they drove. She was perfectly plain, was Emma McBroom. It was the overbite that gave her the look of a rabbit. Her freckled skin was just a shade paler than her light brown hair—she wore it pulled back, exposing large ears with pendulous lobes, like soft, florid fruits—which was just a shade paler than her dress. Clayton wondered what he had ever seen in this small brown woman to make him marry her. But that, he supposed, was one question he ought not to ask.

Home turned out to be a lowly prefab on the edge of town, within scent, if not sight, of the dump. The three sparely furnished rooms were immaculate. No sign of juvenile life, Clayton remarked with relief.

Emma led her husband directly to the bedroom and urged him to lie down. "I've got to get back to work," she said.

Clayton looked at her with his now perpetual expression of befuddlement. He spoke haltingly: "And me? I—don't—work?"

Emma wrinkled her brow as if she, too, were puzzled. Then she sat down on the bed beside Clayton and gently patted his arm. "Honey, you haven't been well enough to work for years."

"Please," Clayton implored her, "tell me what's wrong with me."

But Emma rose and waved her hands in the air, shooing away the possibility of immediate enlightenment. "For heaven's sake, not now, Clay. I've got the whole motel waiting to be cleaned, and then I—" She broke off, smiled slyly to herself, as though at a pleasant secret, and shook her head. "Well, I'll tell you all about that later, too—I promise. Now I think it's best you try to sleep. You look about dead." She stooped, brushed cool, dry lips across his forehead. "Take a bath, why don't you. I did the laundry this morning. Clean clothes in there." She gestured toward the closet as she went out.

She did not return till well after dusk.

While his wife was gone, Clayton went through the house, examining his few and modest possessions. On a pinewood dresser—the only piece of furniture in the bedroom besides the bed—lay a Bible. Clayton opened it and saw his name inscribed on the inside cover in gold. The longer he stared at it, the less familiar the name seemed to him. He riffled the book absently before replacing it on the dresser and going into the kitchen.

In the refrigerator he found a porous, mottled gray slab wrapped in waxed paper. He broke off a crumb and tasted it: meat loaf. Rita's was definitely superior. He sipped some milk from an open carton and immediately afterward felt a prickliness deep in his throat: the never-to-be-slaked thirst that is the chronic symptom of addicts of beer.

In the bathroom Clayton examined his reflection again. It was just as with his name in the Bible: the more he stared, the less familiar his own face seemed to him.

He took a steaming-hot shower and shaved. Cleared of stubble, the scar on his cheek appeared bigger, ruddier, weirder. Whatever could have caused it? That was one of the first things he would ask Emma.

The clothes he took from the closet fit him a bit loosely; evidently he hadn't eaten much in the last two days. Still hungry, he was considering going back to the kitchen to finish off the meat loaf when a wave of fatigue cast him down upon the bed. The next instant he was asleep.

He had a troubling dream, the details of which would later elude him. What endured was the memory of some danger, imminent and grave, and endless miles of obstructed road to be negotiated in order to be safe from it. Some kind of weapon figured somewhere (in later versions of the dream, which would recur often, it was always a pistol). When he woke, the sedan was just pulling up to the house.

Emma entered, looking smaller and browner than Clayton remembered her. Fatigue pinched her face and weighted her movements, but her eyes—which he noticed for the first time were somewhat askew, the right being higher than the left— held a gay, almost mischievous spark. Without taking a rest, she set about fixing a supper of canned ravioli and peas. Clayton sat at the kitchen table and listened as Emma talked.

"I don't know if you remember, Clay, but just before you wandered off, we were talking about finding a new place to live." Needless to say, Clayton remembered nothing of the kind. "Well, this afternoon I drove out to Silver Lake and looked at a place that's just perfect for us. Not that it's anything special— just a little apartment no bigger than this on top of a liquor store. But here's the thing: we can have it rent-free in exchange for my cleaning the store. Now that is one good deal." She looked over her shoulder at Clayton as if to see whether he appreciated this. "Then I checked out the situation for jobs. There are two big lodges on the lake needing maids year-round, and they pay about the same as I've been getting here. So there's no need to worry about work.

"The apartment is ours if we want it. We can move in anytime, and I can't think of a single reason to pass it up. We won't find anything better, and as far as I'm concerned we can't leave here quick enough. Never have liked this town. Cold people—nosy, too." She squeezed her lips into a line. "Never have been much help to us. To hell with 'em."

She plunked an amply laden plate down on the table. This was for Clayton. Herself she served only a fraction as much: two bites and it was all gone. Then she pushed her plate away, leaned her elbows on the table, and continued to talk while Clayton devoured his meal.

This was how it would be every night, first here, then in the new apartment in Silver Lake, to which the McBrooms moved at the end of that week. Emma would come home from work, fix supper, pile Clayton's plate high, eat two bites herself, and talk. Clayton listened as he ate, interrupting his wife often with questions. Thus, little by little, he reacquainted himself with his past.

He'd been born forty-two years before in a town just north of Milwaukee called Algonquin. An only child, he had lost both parents in a single year. His father, whose heart had never been strong, died suddenly; his mother, lingeringly, of stomach cancer. By that time Clayton had finished school. All his life he'd been good with his hands, and he had worked intermittently, as a carpenter and as a mechanic. It was when he was in his twenties that he began to suffer from the mysterious blackouts and fainting spells that made it impossible for him to keep a steady job. He'd seen doctors, of course—a whole hospital of them,

Emma assured him—and not one could help him. Not one could give even a name to what ailed him. Memory lapses were nothing new, but they seemed to be getting worse as Clayton grew older. According to Emma, there was no telling when things would start coming back to him. Maybe a month, maybe a year.

The McBrooms had met at a resort not far from Algonquin where Emma had a summer job as a waitress. On fine days Clayton and his best friend Dean used to drive up to hang out by the lake. Clayton and Emma had their fifteenth wedding anniversary coming up in the fall. Emma reached across the table and squeezed Clayton's forearm when she spoke of this. Seeing her ring, Clayton frowned and held his own, ringless hand aloft. "But what about my ring? What happened to that?"

Emma gasped. Her mouth twisted, and Clayton thought she might cry. "I guess they took it off you," she said at last.

"Who?"

"I don't know. The same ones as stole your wallet, I guess." A shame.

Of course they had wanted children. But, as Emma vaguely put it, this never seemed to happen. Over the years, she had come to think of this lack as a blessing, though. It was hard enough with just the two of them scraping by on her salary.

"That's enough for now," Emma broke off abruptly that first night over supper. "I don't want to tire you. Plenty of time to talk tomorrow." She got up from the table and began clearing away the dishes. But Clayton could not go to bed without asking one last question.

"Tell me, how'd I get this scar?"

Emma hesitated for what seemed to her husband a very long time. She stared at his cheek, as though she herself were having trouble remembering. Finally she said, "That's no scar, Clayton; that's a birthmark. At least, that's what you always told me."

While Emma washed the dishes, Clayton lay in bed staring at

the variously shaped rust-colored stains that covered the ceiling like a map of another world. His fingers strayed repeatedly to his left cheek. Birthmark: it was the last explanation he had expected. He dozed off for a few seconds, waking up again just as Emma was turning out the light. She slipped under the covers and, as she pressed her body against his side, there burst into Clayton's thoughts the image of another woman, naked and beautiful, with a tumble of wheat-blonde curls. Clayton caught his breath. Emma pressed against him, this time more insistently. Still holding the blonde before his mind's eye, Clayton made love to his wife.

That summer in Wisconsin was particularly moist and cool. For Clayton, one day followed another, all much alike. He got up late, at least an hour after Emma had already left the house, and made a breakfast of coffee and toast. Then he turned on the television. In the morning there were several game shows and old sitcoms that he liked to watch, but the midday soaps drove him back to bed for a nap. Afternoons he usually devoted to tidying the little apartment or tinkering with various appliances. Emma was right: he was good with his hands; but there was precious little for those hands to do. Luckily, idleness agreed with Clayton. And, overworked though she was, Emma did not begrudge her husband his life of Riley. If she had a complaint it was that he kept too much to himself. It was true: Clayton shied away from people. How explain a crazy problem like his to other people? Much easier to avoid them. But Emma wanted to make friends, at least with the neighbors, whom she pronounced a cut above the trash they had known in Schocken. And she warned Clayton that it would do him ill, staying cooped up in the house all day with no company, no air.

In time, Clayton ventured out and discovered that he really did enjoy an afternoon stroll down Main Street. And he had no trouble at all chatting with, say, ancient Mr. Braun, the retired baker, who talked mostly about the weather; or with the liquor store owner's wife, who talked only about her cats.

By summer's end, Clayton had gained enough confidence to hang out at Whitey's, a pub at the north end of Main Street, across from the abandoned railroad depot. Whitey's was never crowded before dusk, and, among its lone, taciturn regulars, Clayton felt more or less at ease. He wasn't looking to strike up a friendship, but he liked to watch a ball game in the company of other men, and he liked his beer. Whitey's was the perfect place to while away the hour or so before Emma came home from work.

All in all, it was not a bad life, and Clayton would not have said that he was unhappy. True, he never quite lost that feeling he'd had, from the moment he woke up in the manure-strewn pasture, of falling through space. But as time passed he seemed to be losing velocity: instead of plunging headlong, he was now sinking through space—a far more tolerable sensation. He was grateful for the comforts his wife provided. Emma took care of everything; he never even saw the bills. The only thing she asked in return was that he make love to her, and though he did not desire her, night after night Clayton obliged. He shut his eyes against the plainness of his wife, and night after night the woman with the wheaten hair opened her arms to him.

Clayton had discovered that, if he heard certain experiences described often enough, he came close to feeling as though he could actually remember them. And so he was forever pestering his wife for stories. Happily, Emma took keen pleasure in this pastime and never refused, even when asked to repeat the same things over and over.

Among the stories Clayton liked to hear was one in which he figured as hero, saving a girl from drowning in the lake at the resort where he and Emma had first met. Emma herself had witnessed this feat from the shore, having rushed from the restaurant along with most of the customers at the sound of the girl's cries for help. She hadn't even stopped to put down the platter of fried fish she was carrying. Men had applauded and women had wept as they beheld Clayton walking out of the lake with the girl in his arms. And Emma had made up her mind that she loved him. Later that summer, on the night of a fierce storm, she dreamed that it was she whom Clayton saved from drowning. A clap of thunder woke her just as he was laying her down on the shore. Then the telephone rang and it was Clayton himself, wanting to know how she was managing in the storm. Emma burst into tears and confessed that she loved him. Through darkness, wind, and rain—all the way from Algonquin—Clayton drove that night. By morning, he had asked Emma to marry him.

Every time he heard this story, Clayton was struck with wonder. In the midst of his pride at his valiant behavior, he couldn't help asking himself why he had proposed. For he was quite sure Emma had never been attractive to him, not even fifteen years before.

"Tell me about Dean," Clayton would ask. "The one I used to hang out with. What was he like?"

And for the hundredth time, Emma would describe his old friend: "Good-looking as hell and twice as conceited. Didn't just think he was God's gift to women; thought women were God's gift to him. Smart girls preferred you, though. I always said it was because you were the better man, and it showed. You two were inseparable. He was a bit older, and you sort of looked up to him—you know, like the big brother you never had."

"And whatever happened to him?"

Emma shrugged. "Who knows? He was a drifter. Just up and disappeared one day. Not even a postcard since." The more they talked about Dean, the more Clayton missed him.

One day Emma heard Clayton singing in the shower. He had a fine, deep-chested baritone. When he came out of the bathroom, she told him something she had just remembered: as a teenager, he had won a singing contest sponsored by a Milwaukee radio station.

Clayton was delighted. "Well, how do you like that? What did I sing?"

Emma screwed up her face in the effort to remember. " 'Mona Lisa' I think you said it was."

"Isn't that interesting," said Clayton, shaking his head. "And now I can't even remember how it goes."

Emma attempted a few bars in her feeble voice but wavered so pathetically she had to break off, and she and Clayton both burst out laughing.

Clayton also liked hearing about the time another woman had tried to steal him away. At first mention of this incident, Clayton felt a surge of excitement. He urged Emma to describe her rival, thinking of the woman with the wheat-colored hair.

"Well, I wouldn't say wheat-colored," Emma grumbled. "Dirty blonde is what it was. I should know: my fists were full of it when I was finished with her."

The thought of his meek little rabbit of a wife coming to blows with another woman was too much for Clayton; he laughed until his eyes were moist. "Think that's funny, do you?" Emma sniffed; but there was a gleam in her eye, too.

Oh, but it wasn't all stories and laughter with the McBrooms. From time to time, Emma and Clayton fought. Usually it began with her snapping at him about something she didn't like, such as his habit of leaving used toothpicks lying about. Sometimes it ended right there, but other times some demon would goad Emma to a real tirade. Well, Clayton McBroom was not going to take that from his wife, even if she did support him. And so it happened—not often, thank God, but more likely if he'd been drinking—that Clayton's temper got the better of him, and before he knew it, his belt was in his hand and Emma was all arms, vainly trying to protect herself.

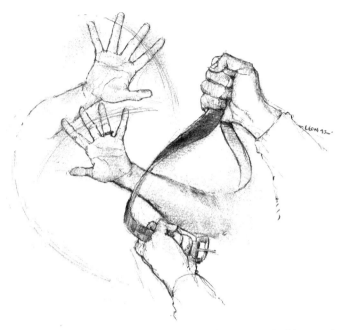

But neither husband nor wife was the sort to hold a grudge, and it was rare that they didn't make up their quarrel before bedtime.

And there were days when the weight of his loss bore heavily upon Clayton, and he grieved deeply for all that he had lived but could not bring back to mind. He wept when Emma told him about the fire. It had started in the wires of the old house, and before the firemen brought it under control, had destroyed, among other things, boxes of photographs and other mementos.

Two photographs remained. Almost every day Clayton took a minute to study the black-and-white snapshot of his parents: an ordinary-looking, middle-aged pair embracing on a love seat. The other snapshot was of Clayton himself, aged five: Halloween; Hiawatha. Feathers and war paint obscured his features so that you could hardly see the child, let alone any resemblance—though Emma insisted you could tell who it was at a glance.

Seeing how sad Clayton was when she brought up the fire, Emma asked him whether he'd like sometime to visit Algonquin, the town where he was born. Clayton said he would like nothing better, and so, one Saturday morning in early fall, they made the three-hour drive.

Algonquin was a quiet, well-tended village with a beautiful antique carousel adorning its main square. Emma drove once around the square, then turned up a hill, bringing them into a neighborhood of large handsome houses set well apart. Clayton held his breath as they pulled up before an imposing greystone structure flanked by tall elms. This was it: his boyhood home. Clayton felt a sudden smarting in the back of his nose. He would have given anything to see the inside, but Emma suspected that the current owners would not be friendly to such a request. Clayton sighed. He would have settled for a glimpse of the backyard, where doubtless he had played every day as a child. And he wondered aloud whether he'd been lonely, without brothers or sisters. Then he remembered one of the few things Emma had told him about her own childhood (in general, Emma was as tight-lipped about her own past as she was talkative about his): she had grown up in a Catholic foundlings home. Clayton reached over and took his wife's hand, and together they beheld the splendid house in silence. Then the front door opened and a man with a magazine rolled in one hand appeared. He stood akimbo and stared at the idling dove-gray sedan. Clayton slunk a few inches down in his seat, and Emma stepped on the gas.

Before leaving Algonquin, they visited the cemetery where Katherine and James McBroom lay buried, side by side. Here and there along the gravelled paths, clusters of wild pinks bloomed. Clayton gathered a small bouquet and laid it between the two graves.

All the way back to Silver Lake, Clayton glowed with thoughts of his happy childhood—for it seemed impossible that a child would not have been happy growing up in such a wonderful house. He thought of the backyard, imagining so clearly a sandbox and swing set he could have sworn he was in fact remembering them. If only he could step inside the house—who knew what memories might come flooding back to him! According to Emma, Clayton's father (a prosperous car dealer) had had to sell the house to help pay Katherine's medical bills. What money remained James had bequeathed to his son—and that, too, ended up in the pockets of doctors. A pity.

They visited the house three more times before the end of that year. It worked like a charm when Clayton was particularly despondent; just seeing the house perked him up.

About a week after the fourth trip to Algonquin, Clayton was having a beer at Whitey's when a man he didn't think he'd seen before came in and sat down at the bar. Nodding at Clayton, the man whistled softly and said, "That was a close one, huh?"

It was a moment before Clayton realized that the man was referring to his birthmark. "Oh, this," he said, self-consciously touching his cheek. "I was born with that."

The stranger cocked his head and eyed Clayton incredulously. Then he shrugged. "If you say so, buddy. I could have sworn it was a bullet wound. I've seen enough of 'em to know. I was a medic in the service."

Turning away at that moment to beckon the bartender, the stranger missed the effect of his words, which was a pallor so intense the mark on Clayton's cheek stood out redly, like a fresh brand. Without finishing his beer, Clayton got up and left the bar.

Back at the apartment, he could not stop thinking about the stranger at Whitey's. And when he thought about what that man had said, he could not help also thinking about the nightmares. They plagued him often, at least several nights a month, sometimes several nights in a row. Of these dreams Clayton never remembered the plot, only a few details and the agonizing air of panic and dread which stayed with him into daylight. He was always in flight; a gun appeared, changed hands, went off. In fact, that was usually when Clayton woke up, drenched and trembling: when the gun went off.

From the first, Clayton had been troubled by the suspicion that these bad dreams were about something that had actually happened. He couldn't say why; it was just a feeling he had. He'd always called that scar a birthmark, Emma said, but that explanation had never sat quite right with Clayton. And now the stranger's remarks made him wonder whether he had told Emma the truth. He remembered how his pulse had quickened when the woman in the green Chevy said the word *sheriff*. Whatever the reason for this—and it seemed to Clayton there must be a damn good reason—he had forgotten it, along with everything else he had once known about himself. What could have happened? Clayton spent the rest of that afternoon brooding.

But to dwell too long on this question was to drive himself mad, so Clayton tried hard to put the stranger and his words from his mind. In time he succeeded—not wholly, but enough to allow his life to resume its lulling pace. Had the tenor of that life had a sound, it would have been like the faint drone of a bluebottle.

Clayton had just finished breakfast. He rinsed his dishes in the sink and sat down in front of the television. When the picture came on he saw that he was tuned in to a talk show. A man and a woman sat facing each other in low-backed swivel chairs that looked too small for them. Clayton was about to switch channels when he caught a word that made him stop, his hand extended toward the dial. It was the word *amnesia*. The man was speaking.

"Of course, there is another type of amnesia that is not caused by injury or disease but is purely psychosomatic. In cases of hysterical amnesia, a person will protect himself against memories too painful to bear by repressing them completely. In these cases the person forgets because he has a compelling psychological need to do so. Amnesia is the perfect defense mechanism. A person can forget everything about himself, even his own identity."

A sudden churn in Clayton's stomach pumped the buttered toast he had just eaten back up into his mouth. Dashing to the sink he could hear the woman's voice saying that she and Dr. Renard would be back after a break.

Shakily reseating himself before the television, Clayton saw a box of detergent dancing with a pair of trousers. He had to sit through several more commercials before Dr. Renard, neurologist, and the show's host returned. But now the discussion had changed. Carefully though he listened, Clayton couldn't quite follow what was being said, but it seemed that Dr. Renard was now talking about the kind of memory troubles old Mr. Braun had. After a few minutes the host thanked Dr. Renard and introduced a young Chinese man holding a violin. Clayton swore aloud and switched off the set.

He pressed his fists to his temples and tried to remember what the doctor had said. Hysterical amnesia, memories too painful to bear, defense mechanism—Clayton could not have strung all the words together exactly as he had heard them, but the gist of Dr. Renard's remarks had definitely hit home. And what if *he* had this kind of amnesia? What if he had done something he had a "compelling psychological need" to forget?

Clayton's head throbbed with dire speculation. Suppose there were some connection between his loss of memory and the scar on his face? Suppose it really were a bullet wound? If anyone were likely to know the truth about this matter, Clayton thought it would be his old buddy, Dean. And he was appalled at how little imagination it took to picture himself and Dean afoul of the law. Together they might have committed a crime. Did *this* explain Dean's abrupt disappearance?

To quiet his nerves, Clayton told himself over and over that he was letting his imagination run away with him. But his suspicions would not be so easily dismissed. He was convinced that he had something to hide. If he wanted proof, all he had to do was think of his dreams. And if those dreams were any clue, whatever it was he was hiding must be very bad indeed.

That evening when Emma came home, she immediately asked Clayton what was wrong, he looked so undone. But Clayton only shook his head; he could not bring himself to tell her. In bed, when she pressed against him, Clayton turned his back to her. He hardly slept that night, so frightened was he of his dreams, and the next day he was a wreck. He couldn't eat, couldn't concentrate on the television. He thought of going to Whitey's early, but was afraid he wouldn't be able to keep down his beer.

The only thing he could think to calm him was a trip to Algonquin. Indeed, the desire to see his old home was so overpowering that by noon he had yielded, even though this meant hitching.

He was lucky: he made the trip in less than four hours and in only three rides. The last ride let him off right at the Algonquin town square.

It was a grilling August day. Under the bright sun the carousel shone; the horses looked sweaty, and the light burning in their glass eyes gave them a wild, panic-stricken expression, as if they were about to stampede.

In spite of the heat and the steepness of the hill, Clayton clipped along, not slowing down until the gray house loomed into view. And as he drew near it, he felt the familiar peace descend on him. The house looked cool in the dark shade of the elms. The rose hedges were in bloom. The air was heady with their fragrance. In the heart of the lawn a sprinkler whirred with giddy recklessness, casting hoop upon hoop of diamonds on the grass.

Clayton sighed. Here, at least, all was as it should be. Something like a huge fist inside him gently unclenched and, for the first time since the morning before, his breath came and went freely.

A large yellow Labrador trotted along the sidewalk in Clayton's direction. He reached out to pet it, but, with a sniff at his knees, the dog trotted on without stopping. Turning back to the house, Clayton thought of the man with the magazine who had chased him and Emma away with his hard stare. The memory made him self-conscious; he dug his hands in his pockets and slouched. Unwise to go on standing there as if he were casing the place, he reasoned. On the other hand, he wasn't ready to go home. Not knowing what else to do, he continued walking up the street.

It really was the nicest town. It really was the nicest neighborhood, with its roomy old houses and broad, elm-shaded streets—a good place to raise children. It was the sort of neighborhood where Sally Miller and her family might live, and so they did.

Here was Sally Miller now, getting out of her car with a load of groceries in her arms.

They saw each other at exactly the same moment. For a few seconds neither spoke. Clayton recognized the woman at once, even twinless, and even before he noticed that the car was the same green Chevy that had stopped for him on the road outside Schocken. As for Sally, she would have recognized the man anywhere. She had often thought of him since that Memorial Day. Indeed, she was not allowed to forget him: every time he saw her leave the house now, her husband warned her not to go and do the same fool thing she'd done that day on her way to her parents' farm. Her ears still rang with the chiding she'd gotten when he first heard the story from the twins.

Recovered from their surprise, Sally and Clayton now smiled at each other, more than a hint of awkwardness in both smiles. Sally shifted her groceries from one hip to the other. "Well," she said. "This is quite a coincidence, isn't it? What brings you to

Algonquin? Don't tell me you live here, too?"

Clayton shook his head. His smile broadened. In spite of his embarrassment, he was glad of this meeting. How nice to be able to tell this kind woman how things had turned out. He would not mention that the sad condition in which she had found him persisted to this very day. But he was pleased to tell her his name and how his wife had rescued him only an hour or so after Sally had dropped him off. Then he jerked his thumb over his shoulder in the direction of the gray house, which was but two doors down from Sally's own, and explained that he had grown up there.

Sally peered down the street, perplexed. "The Swensens'?" she said. "Oh, but you must have the wrong place. The Swensens have lived in that house for three generations. It was built in—" Her voice died away. Had she pulled a knife from her grocery bag and plunged it through his breast, the man could not have looked more aghast. Instantly, Sally was reminded of the look on his face that day on the road when she had asked him his name and he couldn't tell her. Her heart went out to him now, just as it had then, and inwardly she cursed herself. How could she be so thoughtless? The poor man was clearly not of sound mind, and here she'd gone and said something to frighten him.

"Mr. McBroom!" she cried—for he had turned away and was stumbling downhill. Without looking back, he started to run. And Sally would have dropped her bag and run after him—but just then Toby and Tod, who had been shooting baskets behind the house, came hurtling toward her. And one of them (Sally was not sure which) was screaming at the top of his lungs, "Mom, what are you *doing*, talking to that strange guy? Dad'll *kill* you!"

It was after midnight by the time Clayton arrived home. He had left no word as to his whereabouts, and Emma had spent the evening in a state of frenzy. As soon as she saw his face, she knew what was up. Clayton didn't have to ask her to explain; she just started in.

"I knew this day would come sooner or later. I figure I may as well tell you the whole truth right now.

"Your name's not Clayton McBroom. I don't know what your real name is, or who you are, or where you're from. I never set eyes on you till that day at the sheriff's. Clayton was my husband. You know a little about him, because I've told you some things—like how we met at that place on the lake. The only memory troubles *he* ever had was remembering that he was married. Couldn't stay faithful between lunch and dinner. We weren't married more than six months when he took off. That was fifteen years ago, and I haven't seen or heard from him since. It makes me feel almost dirty to say it, but the truth is, I really loved Clayton, and when he left me I thought I would die.

"I kept whatever he didn't take with him: the clothes you've been wearing, those photos I showed you, the Bible—that was a gift from his mother. I kept them, thinking that one of these days he'd be back. Fifteen years: in all that time I don't think I ever completely lost hope.

"Like I told you, I got no family myself. And one thing that's always been true of me is that I'm shy about making friends with people. Clayton and I had some friends in Schocken, but they were his friends, really—or so I found out: after he left they didn't want much to do with me. I was so uncomfortable around them anyway. I knew I hadn't done anything wrong, but I couldn't help feeling ashamed. I couldn't face my neighbors. People on Acorn Lane were a nasty bunch. I could hear them whispering and snickering when I went to the store—I know I wasn't imagining it. And even if I am exaggerating a little, one thing's for damned sure: no one was nice to me, no one tried to comfort me. It got so all I wanted to do was hide. I'd come home from work every night and crawl into bed and cry myself to sleep. Without Clayton I was so alone. I tried keeping a dog for a while—a cute little mutt someone left behind at the Schocken Motel. I got real attached to him, but then one day he ran away, just like Clayton. But a dog can only give a person so much anyway. Even when I had him, there were times I thought I'd go out of my mind if I didn't find someone to talk to. In all these years I never could get used to living like that. I tell you, it's the loneliest feeling in the world.

"And then that Memorial Day on my break between jobs, I was having coffee at the diner when the deputy comes in and starts telling Rita about this man with amnesia. And Rita asks him to describe the man, and well, I swear, except for the scar it could have been my Clayton. I was sitting at the end of the counter by the cash register. I knew the deputy hadn't really seen me. I'm that sort: people look right at me and later they don't remember me—I've always noticed that. Anyway, listening to the deputy, I thought it could be Clayton he was talking about and I knew I had to go find out. So I finished my coffee and went straight to the sheriff's. And no, you weren't that no-account husband of mine, but when I saw you sitting there all forlorn with that pitiful sandwich, I thought, What harm was there in my taking you home? Better than a jail cell, I said to myself.

"Believe me, I've never done anything so crazy in my whole life. As soon as we got in the car I started to panic, wondering how I was going to get away with it. I got us out of Schocken as fast as I could before anyone could get suspicious. I was so unhappy there anyway, I was itching to leave. I thought maybe it could be a fresh start for us both. I promised myself I'd take good care of you, and I did. I didn't think it would be forever. I knew that sooner or later you'd find out the truth, but I kept telling myself I'd deal with that when the time came. Besides, what else could I do? I couldn't exactly bring you back to the sheriff's. Who knows what he might have done to me?

"And then came all your questions, like what happened to your ring, and where did you get that scar—if you knew how hard it was trying to answer all those questions as fast as you kept shooting them at me! I mixed things together—things I knew about Clayton's life with things I made up. It would be hard for me to sort it all out now. Every day while I was doing my vacuuming, I'd try to think about something else I could tell you. After a while I got into it—it even got to be kind of relaxing. But the best part was telling it all to you. It's fun having somebody listen so close to what you say. And it really didn't seem to matter that I was making it all up, since you didn't have any memories of your own. But I always had to be afraid of saying the wrong thing. That was true what I told you about the fire: Clayton and I lost half of what we owned. But I never would have mentioned it if I'd known it was going to make you cry. That's when I got the idea of taking you to Algonquin.

"Clayton was born there. Those are his parents buried in that cemetery. But they lived in a dump, the McBrooms—they were real poor. I didn't see the point in showing you some old shanty, so I drove up that hill and stopped at the first pretty house, that's all. You seemed so taken with that gray house, I didn't see the harm.

"Like I say, I never kidded myself. Sooner or later I knew this moment would come, and I'd be sitting here facing you like this, telling you the truth, and praying that, hoping that—oh!"

Emma, who all this time had been sitting across the kitchen table from the man she could no longer call Clayton, suddenly jumped to her feet and started backing toward the bedroom door. For he had erupted from his chair and stood gripping the table between both hands, as if he would lift it and bring it down on her head. "You . . . you went there . . . you went there to that sheriff's office . . . and you . . . you picked me up . . . you took me home . . . like . . . like I was a puppy from the pound!" And before he knew it, his belt was in his hand and Emma was all arms trying to protect herself.

He beat her till his own arm stung. Then he threw down the

belt and ran from the house.

He tore up Main Street, past the closed, darkened shops—past Whitey's, also dark at this hour—toward the old railroad depot, where a single dull lamp illuminated a crumbling stone bench in a cone of brassy light. Here he threw himself down to catch his breath. The swarm of insects beating wildly about the lamp was like an image of his agitated thoughts.

He was not Clayton McBroom. The happy childhood in Algonquin. The greystone house with its roses and elms. Katherine and James. The lake where he had hung out with Dean—his old pal Dean! He had been missing a best friend he had never even met. He had laid flowers on the graves of perfect strangers. He had wept for the loss of another's mementos, and nightly bedded another's wife. His pride had fed on deeds never done: he had never saved a girl from drowning, had never won a talent contest with his rendition of "Mona Lisa." Tonight, his entire life had been wrenched from him—for the second time. He had been resurrected, only to die again.

All that remained, more intense than ever, were his fears. He thought of his scar, the surging of his pulse at the word *sheriff*, the nightmares, the words of Dr. Renard. This alone had not changed: the fear that he was a wanted man.

Who was he and how came he to be as he was? All the questions answered by Emma were now open again. She was not his wife. Did he have a wife?

All at once, like a mermaid breaking the surface of a lake, the beautiful wheat-blonde woman exploded in his mind. And, as always before her image, the man trembled with pleasure, and this time that pleasure was mingled with hope. *This* might be his wife. This goddess might be waiting somewhere for him. Why, all manner of wonderful things might be waiting for him. The scar: suppose he had been wounded in battle? He might be a war hero. He might be a rich man, a man to be reckoned with. He might be *somebody*.

Giddy with these speculations, high among the stars (which shone especially brightly that moonless night), the man threw up his hands—and a glimpse of them in the harsh lamplight brought him swiftly back down to earth. He had the permanently black cuticles and sinewy forearms of a laborer. It was not such hands as these that touched fortunes, or the reins of power, or the breasts of women the likes of which you saw only in magazines.

Something rustled along the weed-choked tracks. The man knew that it was only some small animal—a raccoon, probably. Nevertheless, he went cold with fear, and when the animal turned its snout toward him and he saw its coal-like eyes glowing greenly in the dark, he cried aloud, as if it were the Devil himself approaching.

But it was only a raccoon. Startled by the man's scream, it fled.

And fled, too, with that scream was the man's last droplet of strength. Cold, frightened, spent, he longed to be back at the apartment. He thought of Emma, and only now did it occur to him that the whole time he was beating her, she had not made a sound. He had left her in a heap on the kitchen floor. He pictured her cowering in some corner of the apartment, twisting her hands as she always did when she was distraught. He thought of those hands, raw from scrubbing. He thought of the food she piled on his plate every night, and of the small brown body she pressed against him in bed.

Why had he beaten her? Now that he thought about it, he felt no anger toward her. After all, hadn't she been good to him? And hadn't they gotten along? Angry at Emma? He shook his head. No, he wasn't angry at all. He must go back to the house and tell her that.

He went back to the house and into the bedroom, where Emma had already cried herself to sleep. He slipped under the covers beside her and he slept, too. In the morning Emma rose as usual and went to work, and when she came home she found him waiting for her. As usual after having beaten her, he

108   *Glimmer Train Stories*

apologized, and as usual she blushed and batted the air with one hand, meaning that she had accepted his apology, even before the words were out of his mouth. Then she set about fixing their supper. For the first time since the day they had met, they ate in silence. And in that silence, all was forgiven and settled between them.

William Styron

WILLIAM STYRON

Pulitzer Prize-winning novelist

Interview

by Melissa Lowver

With the publication of his first novel in 1951 at the age of 26, William Styron established himself as one of the leading authors of his generation. He has written four full-length novels: **Lie Down in Darkness, Set This House on Fire, Confessions of Nat Turner,** and **Sophie's Choice;** a novella, **The Long March;** one play, **In the Clap Shack;** and a memoir called **Darkness Visible,** which chronicles his 1985 struggle and recovery from debilitating, near-suicidal depression.

William Styron

Mr. Styron has won numerous awards, including the Pulitzer Prize, the American Book Award, the Howells Medal, and the Edward MacDowell Medal. He lives in Roxbury, Connecticut, and Vineyard Haven, Massachusetts. He has been married to Rose Styron since 1953, and they have four children.

LOWVER: *In an interview with Peter Matthiessen and George Plimpton in 1954, you cited the Bible as one of the works that influenced the emotional climate of your writing. What was it about the Bible that affected you?*

STYRON: Although I was never religious, then or now, I do

think that the Bible—since I was exposed to it very strongly as a young person, in both growing up in a moderately religious household, and going to school where Bible was required in the curriculum—I learned a great deal about it. I think, at its best, it's a remarkable chronicle with great poetic overtones, and therefore, really a major work of literature. I seem to regard the Bible as literature, and to that extent, I think it has had a great deal of importance in my work.

In that same interview, in comparing emphasis on character or on story, you said that "it takes an extrovert like Dickens to make flat characters come alive. But story as such has been neglected by today's introverted writers." Could you elaborate on that, on the difference between an extroverted and an introverted writer?

Well, I don't know if that holds up as strongly now as then. I mean, there is a strong trend in modern literature known as "post-modernism," which tends to minimize a story and character—in terms of profound introspection—and that kind of writing I'm neither terribly attracted to nor do I want to write. I think that the traditional writing I admire is writing that has a narrative thrust, and a narrative momentum, and also has believable characters. I subscribe to that mode of fiction as being to my mind the most interesting.

Can you use those terms to characterize the young writers of today?

I honestly don't know, because I'm not that attentive to the younger writers. I think that the ones I have read recently are more traditional than the other way around. It seems to me that narrative, the telling of a story, a transparent narrative is still a very strong mode in the writing of fiction.

You have expressed in the past a belief in Hemingway's statement that a writer writes on the basis of the experience of his first twenty-five years. How do you feel about that today?

Oh, I think that there's probably a great validity in that. I do believe that you store up an enormous amount of experience in those first twenty-five years, and that you draw upon that so-called deposit in the bank for a long time afterward. I believe that it is open to other forms of interpretation, but I do think that that's still pretty valid.

I really don't know. I think that any major issue is something that writers will be attracted to. It's part of the function of writing, to address oneself as a writer to large issues. I don't mean to say that every writer has to do that, but it does seem to happen. I would say that the environment is certainly one that seems to be what writers are dealing with at the moment, and I would think that as time goes on, especially a thing like AIDS will be a compelling sort of subject—

—that you think writers will address in their novels?

I would think so, yes. Because anything that intrudes on human experience in a kind of catastrophic way, whether it's a war, or an epidemic, or whatever, is likely to attract writers' attention.

In an interview with Herbert Juin in 1962, you called Set This House on Fire*'s Mason Flagg "the typical American, materialistic and without history." Using that definition, can the typical American be a good writer?*

I don't know if that's a question I can answer. I don't think the typical American can be necessarily a good anything, because we're talking about people who write, or create—if they're good!—and they are, by definition, special people. They're not typical of anything.

I read about the southern tradition that you grew up with, and it seems that many creative people come from some strong, traditional back- ground. Would you say that that's true?

I don't know if you can nail it down that easily. Certainly, there's a southern tradition of writing, which has yielded enormous fruits in terms of the amount of writing that's come from the South. And it has been strong enough to become almost dominant in its time. You could say at the same time that Jewish writing comes from a traditional background, if you want to call it that, and it has had enormous impact on American literature. So, up to a point, I think you could say that it's true. But despite the very great strengths of these traditions as contributory to writing, I don't think you can exclusively say that good writing comes from that.

Also from Set This House on Fire, *Cass discovers, for an instant, a "continuity of beauty in the scheme of all life which triumphs even to the point of taking in sordidness and shabbiness and ugliness." Many of your novels' characters don't seem to overcome ugliness for more than fleeting moments. Do you see that as inevitable for people in general or only inevitable in terms of the points of view and experiences of the characters you've chosen to draw?*

Oh, I think the two are sort of interchangeable with me. I mean, I don't think I can separate my characters from my own feelings about life. I think that if I reflect that sordidness and shabbiness or whatever it's called, it's because I think that life is often a trial for people, and problematical as to whether it's all worth the candles, for many people.

Do you have any current interest or project in the works?

Yes, I do, as a matter of fact, but that's something I'm rather hesitant to discuss. I finished, as you may know, a book I wrote about my experience with depression—and I'm now back on a novella, a short novel about something very close to me. I can't really divulge what it is—I'm working very hard on it, and am hoping it will be done soon. I find myself interrupted more than I should like by things like writing speeches, which I accept doing, and then, all of a sudden when the time comes to write them, I'm usually terribly unhappy because I've accepted something that interrupts my other life. But that's the way it goes.

It seems that your writing method is very strenuous: from the way that you've described how you write your fiction—the getting in touch with your subconscious, the psychological state you've described—is it still a struggle?

Yes, it doesn't come easy for me, and it never has. I've

reconciled myself to that fact, that it's a terrible chore, more than a chore, it's a real act of extreme pain for me to write, but I can't do anything about it because that's the way I'm constituted, I have to deal with it. I suppose I would have written more had it come more easily, but I guess I have to be satisfied with what I've done.

You certainly don't deal with easy issues. There are a lot of things you delve into that I think other writers would find pretty gut-wrenching to explore.

Well, yes, I take some pride in saying to myself that I have not avoided, I've not sidestepped subjects that other writers may have not wanted to tackle. So maybe I've compensated to a degree in that way, by dealing with large themes, and that makes up for the relative lack of abundance. Anyway, time will tell.

What about The Way of the Warrior—*do you still consider that a work-in-progress?*

Well, I'm still working at that—I don't know if it's going to develop. It is still a viable project, and I'm going ahead with it, from time to time. I think it will eventually become something.

How do you feel today, when you sit down in front of that blank piece of paper? Is it ever a friend, or is it mostly an adversary?

Well, it's an adversary that becomes a friend, put it that way. I mean, it starts out adversarial, and as you deal with it—of course, I'm speaking only for myself, not for any other writer—as I deal with it, all of a sudden there's a kind of embrace that takes place, and usually after the struggle to get into something, I find that it gets easier, and, in fact, even enjoyable at times. It's kind of unusual.

MELISSA LOWVER is a longtime employee of ESPN, the cable sports network. Avid outside interests have led her to apply much of her spare time to free-lance research and writing projects. She has also contributed articles to *New England Point of View*, a television and film trade magazine.

Siobhan Dowd, program director of PEN American Center's Freedom-to-Write Committee, writes this column regularly, alerting readers to the plight of writers around the world who deserve our awareness and our writing action.

Writer Detained: Gustavo Guzman
by Siobhan Dowd

*B*ounded by the Pacific, Peru, and Colombia, Ecuador is an impoverished country of some ten million people, mainly of Amerindian descent, who live mostly in the sierra uplands of the Andes or on the coast with its coffee, banana, and cacao plantations. For many years, the country was ruled by military dictatorship; but, in 1979, an academic and Christian Democrat named

Gustavo Guzman

President Osvaldo Hurtado led the country to civilian rule by introducing a new constitution providing for a directly elected president with a nonrenewable four-year term. Voting was declared obligatory for all literate citizens over the age of eighteen—but, given the country's high illiteracy rate, especially among the indigenous peoples (few of whom speak Spanish, the official language), much of the population is perforce excluded from the electoral process. The high illiteracy rate is reflected in the fact that the country's twenty-two newspapers only have a total circulation of about half a million.

Democracy of a kind prevailed throughout the 1980s, but the government appeared to have little control over the police and armed forces. Disturbing reports of arrests of community leaders, beatings and killings of villagers (including children), anonymous death threats, and of torture of detainees held by the Servicio de Investigaciones Criminales (CIS) persisted. Finally, late last year, the government effectively froze the CIS after a human-rights commission conclusively proved that two teenagers, whose mutilated bodies had been discovered at the bottom of a lake, had been arrested, tortured, and killed by CIS officers. The government has since pledged to press charges against officers accused of such abuses, but the judicial process is laborious and highly sensitive politically.

The case of Cesar Gustavo Garzon Guzman, a writer who was especially passionate in denouncing the victimization of Ecuador's indigenous population, is one of the many that remain unresolved. To this day, it is unclear if and how he died, or if he is lying in an unmarked grave, at the bottom of a river, or, as now seems less and less likely, in a prison cell. The CIS was suspected by Guzman's associates of having abducted him, but its effective dissolution has provided no clue to Guzman's whereabouts and the hopes of ever finding him alive are thus all but dead themselves.

Guzman was only thirty-two at the time of his disappearance in 1990. He was born in Quito, the country's capital, and, after graduating from a local high school, he studied statistics and banking at the Central University of Ecuador. He presumably

116   *Glimmer Train Stories*

discarded all thought of a business career at some point in his early twenties, for, by the age of twenty-five, he had started to publish his writings in several magazines, including *Libro de Posta*. From 1984 to 1987, he was coeditor of a magazine called *La Mosca Zumba*. He also enrolled at the Pontifical Catholic University of Ecuador to study for a doctorate in literature; his dissertation was apparently well under way at the time of his disappearance.

He also became active in leftist politics and, in 1989, in the midst of an election campaign which he believed was irrelevant in terms of alleviating the exigency of Ecuador's indigenous population, he joined a group of radical-thinking friends on a tour of rural communities. His aim was to gather facts and figures about the miserable conditions in which his fellow citizens lived, and the result was the creation of a sardonic and angry collection of short stories he entitled *Brutal como el Rasgar de un Fosjer (Brutal like the Striking of a Match)*. The stories—an unusual blend of self-analysis, surrealist verse, and fable—are Kafkaesque in their effect. In an extract from one of them, "Zero Hour," he asks himself in despair what he can do about the poor:

> Another line on the palm of the hand, and the palm says: What can I do?
> What can I do if the poor are still poor?
> If I cannot have a spirit because the poor are still poor?
> What can I do if the beauty of words
> of sounds
> of colors
> Or the beauty of a woman does not exist because the poor are still poor?
> What can I do if my momentary happiness is not the happiness of those who are still poor?

His activities apparently displeased CIS officers and, on his return to his home province, he was arrested. Guzman later claimed to have been tortured while in incommunicado detention. He was charged with "illegal association" for his alleged links with a Marxist guerrilla organization called Montoneros Patria Libre. He was held for thirteen months, during which time Amnesty International adopted him as a prisoner of conscience, and was eventually freed after a judge dismissed the charges against him. His friends report that his time behind bars tempered his activist ardor somewhat, and he vowed to devote himself in future to writing rather than to radical politics.

A few weeks later, he received a fee for his first book, his 1989 collection of short stories, from the publishing house Editorial El Conejo. It was presumably in good spirits therefore, with everything in life to look forward to, that he went out the following night, November 9, 1990, to the Sor Candela disco in Quito to celebrate a friend's birthday. He left in the small hours of the next day and was never seen again.

The police denied having arrested him, although most of his friends and family believe that his disappearance was arranged by the CIS in an effort to spite the judge who had dismissed the case against him. His mother, Clorinda Guzman, writes to PEN: "On November 10, a search was made among his family and friends; the next day the search was extended to hospitals, clinics, the Center of Preventative Detention, the local jail for men, and even the morgue of the National Police." On November 14, Guzman's fellow students announced his disappearance on the radio and in the press. Over the next weeks, his mother continued to bring up her son's case with various government officials. Testifying before Ecuador's Constitutional Court, she declared angrily: "Disappearance is one of the most sinister and subtle mechanisms which the government employs to appear democratic while repressing those who fight for the higher interests of our people."

After his disappearance, his stories were published (probably, alas, posthumously). In one story, "Instinct on the Alert," Guzman predicted correctly the dangers he would face, but expressed an assurance, apparently unjustified, that he would safely weather them: "My watchman is me," he wrote. "I am my own guard and no bullet-proof jacket or gust of wind can blow away the truth of the wick that burns in the core of my being."

In her letter to PEN, Clorinda—who refers to her son's age as thirty-two, despite the fact that, if alive, he would now be thirty-four—concludes: "This is all I can tell you about the disappearance of my son and the subsequent transactions. Unfortunately, I have had no further news about him. The only thing I can hope for now is that through you I will find out what happened to my son, Gustavo."

Letters supporting Clorinda's tragic search for the truth, which necessitates that all avenues continue to be explored in the investigation into Gustavo Guzman's disappearance, that any findings be made public, and that those responsible for any harm that has come to him be brought to justice, can be sent to:

> His Excellency Rodrigo Borja Cevallos
> Presidente de la Republica del Ecuador
> Palacio Nacional
> Garcia Moreno 1043
> Quito
> Ecuador

Thanks are due to Mandy Garner of PEN for the translation of extracts from Guzman's work.

Elizabeth Judd

Elizabeth Judd's short stories have been published in *The Agincourt Irregular* and *New Mexico Humanities Review*. Her nonfiction book, *Investing with a Social Conscience*, was published by Pharos Books (New York) in August 1990. Judd's nonfiction has appeared in the *Voice Literary Supplement*, the *Ann Arbor News*, *Paris Passion,* and several business-oriented publications. She is currently writing a novel, which is "tentatively entitled" *Anna Jupiter.*

In May of 1992, Judd graduated from the M.F.A. Creative Writing Program at the University of Michigan. Since then, she has moved to Philadelphia and is newly married.

ELIZABETH JUDD
Mirrors to the Soul

*P*icasso-eyed, I naturally look at the world differently. One eye charges toward my temple, a Dada eye, large and alert with a sexy tilt at the edge; the other is small and sleepy like the heavy-bellied moon in a nursery rhyme. The overall effect is a fractured, Cubist look.

At seven Jamie Will stopped sending me crayoned hearts pierced through by feathered arrows when I pointed this blossoming defect out to him. "That eye's bigger," he gaped. "Weird." That afternoon Jamie didn't meet me at the playground. And from then on he stared at me like I felt my child self staring at midgets or fat ladies—frozen, unable to look away.

Many years later my husband divorced me because he couldn't bring a pigeon-toed wife to the Upper East Side parties he was being invited to. Or so I surmised. All he said was that I didn't seem to *fit* anymore.

But now my luck seems to have changed. My love of the last year, Sam Stillings, is an artist and so I can stop guessing which flaws he is secretly storing as ammunition against me since he paints them all plainly in oils. He carves out the gap between my front teeth and builds up the squiggled bump on the bridge of my nose. And of course he paints my two mismatched eyes like oddly set jewels. These deviant features are portrayed with affection and even give my face a rakish daring in his work. But I'm taking no chances. At night I fill in the space between the painted woman's teeth and whittle down her nose to a cover girl pertness. I even out the eyes. I don't think he will leave me.

My affair with Sam seems to illustrate the old adage that practice makes perfect. All prior relationships have led only to this. Take this morning, for instance. There I was, scrambling to catch the Long Island Railroad for my reverse commute, winding through the collision course of paintbrushes soaking in mayonnaise jars and canvases perched on countertops, and there *he was*, snoring face-down into his pillow. A few years ago, I would have dropped the coffee pot on the linoleum floor and let the shriek of glass shattering and the lisp and hiss of hot coffee bathing the cabinets wake him. But not now. Let the Marilyn Monroes of this world cause the scenes; the Lenore Delaneys put their pumps on in the hall so that the clickety-clack of heels doesn't wake their sleeping lovers.

I met Sam through the We-Try-Harder-Rent-A-Car agency where I work as a claims manager. I rarely meet eligible men this way because anyone with a serious enough claim gets turned over to the men behind the oak doors in Counsel. But even though Sam's case was a whopper—he was mistaken for the bank robber whose getaway car he had unknowingly rented and so spent a night in an Arizona jail—he was too sweet to sue and simply wanted the late return charge removed from his bill. The whole thing dragged on for weeks, but I didn't mind. Already, I was more than half in love with his rumbling Irish voice asking for "Mrs. Lenore" on the telephone.

When the check finally came, I called him and he mumbled something about rent past due and coming by that afternoon. It was six before he arrived and the place had cleared like a bomb scare at 4:59. But I knew. I waited. In walked Sam, a big, sexy man with a full beard streaked with white, just like the actor whose name I always forget, the artist who falls for the skinny, rat-faced actress in *An Unmarried Woman*. Well, he asked me out for a drink, and it would take eviction papers to get rid of me now.

I arrive at the office to find pink and blue streamers connecting our desks to the overhead lights, and I remember that today is Maria Mordacello's, our office captain's, birthday. The thing about Maria is that she is a real knockout, with a natural Renoir blush and the feverish coloring the French Impressionists just adored. (I majored in art history at Sarah Lawrence before I dropped out to marry Dumb-Dumb Delaney.) But the tan pancake lines under her chin and the fire hydrant red lipstick blurring her mouth blow the whole picture.

I say, "Happy Birthday, Maria. Which is it, forty-five?" and walk on. Over my shoulder, I add: "Like the Donny Osmond pantsuit. Sharp." And there she is, her teased hair piled high, convulsed in breathless giggles. It's a funny thing but every man I have ever known will devour a compliment, whole, no matter how farfetched it may be. But if I said to Maria, "Looking good, Christie Brinkley," she would have known I was making fun of her, while the truth—mighty tacky pantsuit—is the funniest joke on earth. My theory is that women trust in a social order in which no one would dare say something nasty. Here's the logic: If Maria's outfit *did* make her look ridiculous, I would never have mentioned it. Therefore, my commenting on it either means that I envy her and her pantsuit or at least her outfit is not so bad that it can't be spoken about.

As soon as the four women from Claims sit down for Maria's birthday lunch and order the first round of piña coladas, the conversation takes an ominous turn. Wide-eyed Suzie Miles, straight from the senior prom, says, "So, girls, did you hear about the study by Harvard doctors about single women?"

"No," I say, like the stomp of a foot, hoping to put out the conversation before it flares.

"You know," says Shirley, "my husband died with all his own teeth. Forty-six, and all his own teeth. Not even a single cavity." We all smile politely at her non sequitur. Somehow all of Shirley's stories pivot upon the frozen moment of her husband's death—as if she couldn't quite keep up with the quickly ticking seconds until Ralph's heart attack stopped them forever. "But what survey is this?" she asks, her mind tugged back to Suzie's question.

"Oh, everyone's talking about it," gushes Suzie. "These doctors have been *studying* statistics on marriage for *years*. It seems that a twenty-five-year-old woman who's never been married has only a fifty-fifty chance of *ever* getting married. *And* an unmarried thirty-year-old has a better chance of being killed in a *plane* crash than of marrying."

"A plane crash?" Shirley says. I envision the government subsidizing mercy flights for thirty-year-old women, and I can see Shirley calculating all that dentistry, those natural teeth, going to waste.

"Of course," Suzie says bitterly, tamping a pack of cigarettes on the table, "the whole picture's a lot brighter for men."

"Well, there's always me," says Maria, holding her newly diamonded finger up as a symbol of hope. "Thirty-three today," she says and laughs nervously as one who is about to cheat statistics should laugh.

"Lenawhawhhhr," demands Suzie like an impish emcee.

"What?" I say. "I've got Sam. Remember? And besides I *was* married. Those statistics don't apply to me." With that, I notice the approaching waiter, compressed by a huge tray of seafood specials, and I hope the brightly colored dishes with their green parsley trees and yellow lemon wedges will distract the women from Claims. No such luck.

"Sam?" Suzie sputters. "Artists are penniless. Give that guy the gate."

"You could do better, honey," Maria says, placing her hand over mine.

"The gate," Suzie repeats.

"Yeah, and wait for what? My plane to crash?" I realize I'm shouting, but the women from Claims do not seem to hear. They are now happily pinching the lemons, wringing them, and plopping red pools of ketchup onto their plates.

That evening the windows in our apartment are flung open and the sweet spring air that somehow survives the pollution of New York City has chased the heavy paint smells from the apartment. But no Sam.

I put the chain on the door and wander into his studio for some quick touch-ups. Two new canvases peer at me and I know from the woman's classic beauty that my lover has learned his lesson and now sees as I wish him to see. The light brown hair is a golden glow, smooth and warm. The nose is narrow, the gapless teeth drawn together in a charming smile. But then, uneasily, I see the world—whole—from a new angle. No woman trusts the too extravagant compliment: Sam's even-eyed love is not me.

James English

My father had a good eye, was quick with a camera, and happened to write for Business Week. *I've never looked good in pinstripes.*

James English was raised in Grafton, Massachusetts. He now lives in Providence, Rhode Island, with his wife and three children.

English has published in the *Harvard Advocate*, the *Florida Review*, and (forthcoming) the *Nebraska Review*.

JAMES ENGLISH
Goosewing

*I*t's February, my wife has the flu, and I've been assigned to the roll-out couch in the family room. In the fourteen years of our marriage, I've come to know this couch intimately. Flus. Pregnancies. The children's illnesses. A few Christmases ago, Angela bought me a traveler's alarm clock and an extra pillow.

I'm trying to nudge myself toward drowsiness. It's like launching a rowboat in a shallow pond. Television. The newspaper. Old photo albums. I'm looking at a photo of my wife when she was pregnant with our first child. There is something about a pregnant woman's aura, something flush and lyrical, which arouses me. Angela is on a wide beach, waving a tiny flag. Her stomach swells like some sweet, overripe fruit. Behind her, an elderly couple reposes under a flaring yellow umbrella. The caption reads: "Goosewing. Summer. 1978."

I turn the page. Here is a photo of the two of us, courtesy of some forgotten beachgoer. I am leaning over Angela's shoulder, engulfing her in my arms. She has her hands on my wrists, fending me off. Behind us, the ocean extends forever.

Photos of the rental beach house. The garden. The road to the beach. After we unpacked, we went for a tour. The house was an old, cedar-shingled New England saltbox, but the interior had been elegantly refurbished. There was a dishwasher and disposal in the kitchen, a huge gabled window artfully sliced out of the living room wall, track lighting in the pantry.

The owners, a Hartford surgeon and his wife, had left a note clipped to the refrigerator door. The clip was in the shape of a lobster. "If the upstairs bedrooms get too hot, there's a portable bed in the living room."

While Angela finished unpacking, I toured the backyard. By the garage were two large, blue plastic buckets, half full of rainwater. I brought the buckets into the kitchen, carefully poured them into four separate pots and put the pots on the stove to heat. I found Angela upstairs. "Have you ever showered with rainwater?" We'd been married less than a year. We were novices with each other.

She was wearing shorts and a loose cotton shirt. A shallow film of perspiration delicately moistened her forehead. She looked sensual, wifely. "Never," she said.

I went into the bathroom and turned on the shower. Then I brought up the pots of rainwater. We undressed and stepped into the plastic stall. The water felt cool and bracing. I poured some rainwater on Angela's head, added shampoo, and began lathering. The shampoo burst into glossy, velvety suds. I could have been washing with silk.

"Like it?" I said.

She nodded. I could see her eyes pinched closed, as if she were making a wish.

Angela was eight months pregnant then and she carried the baby low and saliently. She didn't look as if she could be any more expectant if she tried. Neighbors kept asking whether our obstetrician had erred on her due date. I splashed some rainwater across her womb, caressed it with soap, watched the quick and silky lather. Beneath my hand, the baby felt quiescent, hard, determined. "It's not a baby," I'd tease. "It's a melon."

Now, in the shower, I asked her if she felt cooler.

She nodded, her lips pursed.

I asked if we could stay a little longer.

Another nod, but slower, less certain.

"Everything all right?" In the early years of my marriage I thought husbands could pursue whenever they wanted to.

No answer.

A half mile from our rented cottage was a granite and oak sign which said in simple, carved letters: "Goosewing Beach." The first time we drove down the narrow, tree-flanked lane and broke out into a clearing, I saw cows grazing in a hilly meadow. Beyond them was the beach—a quarter mile distant, shimmering bluely in the sunny haze. How exciting the first beach of the year was! The wind streamed noisily through our windows. Far, far out on the water, a handful of sailboats skidded across the green sea.

We parked, gathered our paraphernalia, and walked down a sandy path bordered by dune grass.

"Watch out!" Angela said.

"What?"

"Poison ivy." She pointed at the shiny green leaves growing among the dune grass. "It's everywhere."

The beach was barely two hundred yards long—at least the part protected by lifeguards. Beyond the safety flags, it stretched in both directions in one great, mile-long arc before disappearing behind loamy points of land. Two lifeguards loafed near a dingy elevated chair at the center of the beach. A third was reading a book on a worn-out, stuffed couch inside their rescue hut. People were sprinkled across the sand like decorations on a cake.

Angela had been hot all morning, and the first thing she did was dig a deep, round hole and lie face down, letting her stomach droop into the moist, grainy sand.

I asked, jokingly, if Marki recommended digging holes. Marki was her physician back in Albany.

Angela smiled "No." She lay her head on her hands and closed her eyes. Her breath fluttered the sand.

Neither of us had slept well our first night in the rental house. One of the bedroom windows was jammed closed. A mosquito patrolled the upstairs with exquisite vigilance. Angela was hot, restless, nettled. I remember lying next to her and feeling the heat radiate brightly off her body.

Around midnight she said, "If you could sponge me, it might help."

I got up, found a washcloth, and wet it with cool water. When I returned, she was lying on her side. Slowly, methodically, I

130   *Glimmer Train Stories*

moistened her neck and shoulder blades, her spine, her buttocks, worked my way down her thighs and calves, pulled the heat from the soles of her feet. In birth class, we'd been taught to massage from the torso to the extremities. Angela rolled over cumbrously and I wet her stomach, her breasts, her arms. When I reached her fingers, I tugged at them with the washcloth, tugged at the heat. "That's good," she sighed.

I drew Angela to me and kissed her. I could feel the moisture rapidly drying on her body, like rainwater evaporating on hot pavement. She responded to me, but without urgency. Angela was not a mother, yet she was beginning to feel like one—capacious and protective and dutiful. I sensed that she might be in the mood to make love, but also that she might not, that it was more complicated and entangled than I could know.

I rolled on top of her. Her breath was turgid and labored. I could hear it rustle against my ear. In birth class the instructor had talked about the breath. "Put your hands on your ribs and feel how active your breath is. Your breath is your life," she said. "It's your soul. Focus on your breath."

The baby was between us, hard and obdurate and round, and I felt, as I had for the past several months, that our marriage was changing, that Angela was becoming a different person. I knew this had to happen, but there was something about Angela I hadn't seized and possessed yet. I felt my time was running out. I didn't have my full weight on her, but even so, her hands were on my hips, restraining me, holding me at bay. I kissed her again. And then she said, "Where do you think we'll be in ten years?"

"What?"

"I was just wondering. Do you think we'll still live in an apartment? Do you think we'll have lots of kids?"

I shrugged. The moment was gone. "Who knows?"

Angela sighed. "I bet I'll be fat."

"How do you know that?"

"I don't know. I just do."

After Angela woke from her nap on the sand, I walked down to the water with her. The waves rolled onto the beach and exhaled themselves limply. A gentle wind pushed filaments of spray into our faces. I'm a poor swimmer, but at a pool or a lake I compensate by keeping in the shallow area. Surf frightens me. I closed my eyes and dove through a wave. Angela waded out farther, plunged in, and started swimming with crisp, sculpted strokes.

I pursued her for a few yards, stopped, and tried to touch bottom. I turned and swam back in. "Wait!" I yelled. "You forgot me!" I could feel the wind throw my words back.

Angela waved. Her mouth opened but no sounds came. She waved and I waved. She swam out past the breaking waves, out beyond any other swimmer, and then turned and started to float. She was fifty yards from shore.

I backed out of the surf and walked over toward the lifeguard chair.

Out in the water, Angela floated gently, like some limber, humped vessel. People passed me, carrying Frisbees and radios and Playmate coolers. I wanted to say: "That's my pregnant wife floating out there. Can you keep an eye on her?"

I asked the lifeguard if there were any rip currents. He shook his head. He had a plastic whistle around his neck and a glob of zinc oxide on his nose, but he looked frighteningly young. He was just a boy.

"Who's that out there?" I pointed at my wife. My wife. My unborn child. They were tiny specks in the great, blue ocean.

"I've seen her before," the lifeguard said. His voice was shrill, callow. I was sure he'd never rescued anyone. The lifeguard said, "I think she was here Sunday."

I started to walk back. I looked at where Angela was supposed to be but she was gone. "Hey," I turned around and yelled. "Where did that woman go?"

The lifeguard was re-tying the knot on his whistle. He looked up, but in the wrong direction.

"Hey!" I yelled louder. "That woman! She was right there!" I pointed to where Angela had been. Some people near us turned and stared.

The lifeguard squinted at the spot where I'd been pointing. He nodded. "You mean the floating lady?"

When I looked back, Angela was there. I shook my head. I said to the lifeguard, loud enough for the people nearby to hear, "She wasn't there a minute ago. I was watching." I stressed the *I*.

"That happens," the lifeguard said.

Once, before we were married, I forced myself on Angela. It was only once; I never did it again.

We'd been at a party, and I'd drunk too much, and when we got back to Angela's apartment I asked if I could have a cup of coffee.

At the time, Angela was living with two roommates in Schenectady. Her bedroom was off the kitchen. While she was heating the water, I lay down on her bed. I must have fallen asleep, because the next thing I remembered Angela was turning off the lights and sliding into bed next to me.

I reached over and started massaging her back and buttocks. She was wearing a nightgown. I started to lift it off. She held my wrist lightly, as if it were a bouquet of flowers, and said, "Not tonight, Rocco."

I went back to rubbing her. I felt electric with desire. I felt entitled. I started to peel off her nightgown.

"Rocco. Please."

I kept undressing her. She didn't resist, at least not actively. She was lying on her stomach. I rolled her over. Rolling over an unwilling woman is dreary work. It's like pushing a heavy, wet log. When Angela was on her back, I tried to put my hand between her legs. She demurred. I massaged her breasts, her stomach, her thighs. I felt in a hurry. In the kitchen I heard someone asking for cider and wondering where the oatmeal cookies were. I went back to her thighs. I forced my hand between her legs.

"Rocco," she whispered. She sounded less angry or frightened than she did disappointed. "You're drunk."

"No I'm not."

"Yes. You're drunk."

"All right. I am. So what?"

"So I don't want you like that."

"How do you want me?"

A long pause. "I don't know."

This photo always startles me. It's Angela far out in the water. It was our last time at the beach. The hottest day of the week. It seemed as if the heat had been accumulating for days under a hazy canopy of sky. We set up our umbrellas and blanket close to the lifeguard flags. It was too hard to walk on the burning sand.

The surf was heavy and the waves came rolling onto the beach with a weighty, ominous force. I wondered where the waves came from, what distant disturbances had caused them. I walked in ahead of Angela. I dove through a wave. I swam out ten yards and tried to touch bottom. I couldn't. I turned around and started to swim back.

Angela breaststroked out through the surf slowly, confidently. Whenever it looked as if a wave would break on top of her, she ducked under the surface and glided smoothly beneath it. Just before she went in, she'd patted her stomach and said: "I'll be fine. The baby makes me buoyant."

The previous night I remember waking with the feeling that Angela was staring at me. I turned and looked at her.

"Rocco," she said.

"What's up?"

"I can't sleep."

"Is this it?" I raised myself to my elbows, wondering where I'd

134

put the car keys. Even though she had more than five weeks till her due date, we'd heard several stories about early deliveries.

She shook her head. A pause. "Do we have any peaches left?"

I went downstairs to the kitchen. On the wall was a framed copy of the owners' wedding vows. We'd noticed it our first day. I don't remember the exact words, but it was something like: "Birth, death, and marriage are the three major events in one's life; our births are thrust upon us, we are born to die, but we choose our marriages."

There was a flashlight by the stove and I switched it on. During the daytime, the kitchen was a bright, friendly room, but in the dark the house seemed to revert to a different set of tenants. I found the fruit bowl on the counter by the toaster. On the way back I passed Angela's bathing suit. She'd washed it in the kitchen sink and left it to dry in the pantry. I touched it once.

"You're lucky," I said when I returned. "There was one left."

Angela was sitting up, her knees raised. She took the peach and looked at it appreciatively. "Want any?"

I shook my head. I wanted to go back to sleep.

She took a bite. I could hear her sucking the peach juices so they wouldn't drip. "Rocco?"

I opened my eyes again. Looked at the ceiling.

"That woman was right."

"What woman?" I didn't feel like talking. It would wake me more.

"The one on the beach yesterday, who said it won't be the same after we have kids." She took another bite of her peach. I could hear the juices smacking against her lips.

"What do you mean?"

"After the baby comes. It won't be the same."

Angela took another bite of her peach. More juices. More humble, quiet sucking. I sat up in bed and looked at her.

She'd installed a night-light in the bedroom for her nocturnal trips to the bathroom. It cast a yellowy, pale glow on her. She didn't wear any clothes to bed on those torrid nights and I could see the peach juice dribbling languidly down her chin and onto her breasts, which were full and comely in anticipation of the baby. Angela was getting ready for the baby. She was nesting. She was settling.

Lying in the roll-out bed now, I suddenly feel a fatigue of many years. We have two daughters, and they are the most precious people in the world to us, but it's been arduous and enervating. We're always shuttling them off to dance class, or the orthodontist's, or a friend's house. And then there's algebra, horseback riding, shoes. It hasn't gotten easier as we've become older, nor do we have any more energy. And here's the thing: I still desire my wife, I still feel the same spry randiness and eroticism I felt when we were first married, but I can't reach it. It's as if it were on a high shelf, far above me, in some darkening room. Angela is the same way. A few nights ago she fell asleep reading the newspaper. I watched the slow, steady rising of her shoulders, listened to her in-breath, then her out-breath. I remembered the birth instructor telling us to massage toward the extremities. Your breath cleanses you. Your breath reconstructs you. Focus on your breath.

I look at the last beach photo. "Angela!" I yelled. "Come back!" I motioned with my hands and lips. "You're too far away."

There was no response.

"Come back!" I motioned again.

Out in the green ocean, my wife waved. She patted her stomach. She patted our baby.

Susan J. Alenick

The following, written in my own hand and dated (by my
mother) September 1947, is pasted in the photo album
opposite this picture:

Januery has come again
With all it's snow and Sadness
Thowe spring will come in time ennugh
Then we will have some Gladness.

Susan J. Alenick lives in a big, old house in Burlington, Vermont, where she
quilts, writes, and looks forward, still, to the coming of spring.

Although Alenick has written for in-house and technical publications, as well
as for radio and television, "Chips and Whetstones" is her first published
fiction. She is completing a novel, *Quilt Blocks with Geranium*, of which "Chips
and Whetstones" is one block.

SUSAN J. ALENICK
Chips and Whetstones
(a quilt block)

When the pavers laying my new sidewalk go home at four o'clock, they leave behind one man to guard their work from passersby who might write names or something worse in unset cement. Soon a flock of crows descends to peck between long strands of straw for grass seed hidden by the landscaper. The man ignores them until one bird darts across the sidewalk to feed on the neighbor's blackberry bush. Then he shouts, waves his arms, drives all the birds away, and curses the fine line of crow's feet that mars the pavement square.

In the worst ice storm of the century, a dark winter rain suddenly freezes into paralyzing thicknesses. The destruction is enormous. Trees and power lines are down all over town. Emergency rooms are crowded with victims of falls and car accidents. Thousands are without heat and electricity. My neighbor's slender, young birch tree seems to define our help-lessness as it bows all the way to the ground, frozen in the act of supplication.

But the beauty is also enormous. Trunks and limbs of old maples are completely encased in ice, their smaller branches tipped with frozen droplets like buds from a remembered season. Long, thick icicles hang from all the roof edges, and thin, short icicles dot power lines and accent the grillework of wrought-iron handrails. In one front yard, there is so much ice on the evergreen shrubs and bushes that it fills even the spaces between the plants as if sheets of rain were frozen in midair. On my lawn, every blade of grass has its own shield of ice, and when I walk on it there is a sound like the breaking of fine china.

On the second day after the storm, the sun comes out, but it is still too cold to melt the ice. I drive into the countryside, passing industrial parks and used-car lots that look as if they have been preserved in crystal. I steer between prisms of light shooting across the road from the woods on either side of me. Once, I look up and the hillside in front of me seems like a giant waterfall frozen in its descent. I pull off the road and walk into the forest, thinking that in its stillness I can impose some meaning on all of this. But I've gone only a few steps when a sudden movement in the air sets off a clatter of crackling ice, and I run back to my car and home.

On the third day, the warming front moves in, and the ice begins to melt. The neighbor's birch tree, its prayers answered, rises slowly to full height. I stand beside my lilac bush, expecting to see the ice disappear drop by drop, but I am surprised at how the melting takes place. The ice on top of a branch, nearest the sun, melts first, creating icicles beneath the branch. When the ice on top can no longer support the weight below, it pulls away from the branch and hangs for a time like a scalloped edge. Then it cracks in the middle, breaks, and falls. It is only the ice left at each end of the branch that melts away one drop at a time.

In the Midlands of England, a species of butterfly is preyed upon in its chrysalid stage by ants and other creatures of the field. To insure its survival, the chrysalis secretes a honeylike substance which is so irresistible to the ants that they surround the chrysalis, lapping up the honey and protecting the benefactor from other predators. This relationship continues until the shell of the chrysalis opens and the butterfly emerges, ice blue and free to fly.

I look down from the deck of Natasha's mountain retreat, my attention drawn by an unexpected movement below. In the predawn dimness, I see Othello, Natasha's black Burmese, walking along the path that cuts the forest floor. Though he is a small cat, and looks even smaller from this height, he steps with an aristocratic lightness that pronounces ownership and invulnerability. Below the house, Govinda, the adopted stray retriever, has been playing with an old shoe. Her back is to the path and she doesn't see the cat, but as Othello passes, she stops playing and stares into space, the forgotten shoe dangling from her mouth like a grotesque tongue. Othello moves on. A few minutes later, Govinda is by my side. She looks up at me, then lays her head in my lap, seeking consolation for the loss she cannot name.

"The cows are lying down. It must be going to rain."
I swerve the car.
"What did you say?"
"I said—"
"I heard what you said. But what did you say? What does it mean?"
"It's just a saying. If the cows are lying down it's going to rain. It's just something they say."
"Who says it? Who is they?"
"I don't know. Farmers, I guess. I don't know."
"Is it true?"
"How should I know? Just forget it, Jill. Forget I ever said it."
But I can't forget it. Here is the potential for an absolute. Something true that human thinking and fallibility can't undermine. A natural, if not eternal, truth.

All during craft-show season. Up and down the roads. Selling quilts in Vermont. New York. New Hampshire. Massachusetts.

Looking at fields of cows. Standing cows. Lying-down cows. Looking at the sky. The weather. Rain. Sun. Cows standing. Cows lying down.

Cows on one side of the road standing. Cows on the other side lying down. Will it rain on one side and stop before it reaches the other?

Half the cows on one side of the road standing. The other half lying down. A fifty percent chance of rain? So this is how Stuart Hall forecasts the weather. Not by scientific equipment. Cows. He counts the cows. Half up. Half down. A fifty percent chance of rain. Elementary.

But which half is lying down? How do they know? Age? Color? Breed? Is there a certain time of day when they know? After milking? Or when their udders are heavy and almost scraping the ground? Should they even have udders? Do only boy cows know the coming weather? Should they be neutered boys or sexually active? Before or after having sex?

"It looks like rain, Jill. Shouldn't you take your plastic covers to the show?"

"Let me go out and count the cows. The sexually active four-year-old brown-and-white Guernsey cows."

But is it only cows? What about sheep? Goats? Chickens? In England, a whole field of pigs lying down. But it always rains in England. No animal would ever stand up. Another variable...sexually active four-year-old brown-and-white Guernsey American (or is it only Vermont?) cows.

But one day when the cows are standing, I leave the plastic covers home, and it rains. And when eighty percent of the cows are lying down, I take the covers, and the sun burns cracks into my face. I follow Stuart Hall. He drives from downtown to the TV station and back again, never passing a field of cows. It is a hoax. Just something they say. Another not-truth. In the middle of a drought I take the plastic covers.

And on Labor Day, I drive home from the Sheffield Fair in a

downpour that makes rivers out of cracks in the road. On Dorset Street in South Burlington, I see the Monnettes' brown-and-white cows (the only cows left on Dorset Street) standing in their field looking to the west, their faces beaten by the driving rain. I open the window and shout: "It's raining, you idiots! You should be lying down!"

Two miles later, I turn onto Williston Road. Turn left toward Burlington. Turn to the west. Turn...at exactly the moment the first ray of sun pierces the thinning clouds above the Adirondacks.

At a quilting workshop, a lecturer speaks on the science of color. When light hits an object, she says, some color rays are absorbed while others are reflected back. It is the reflected color that we see and name. A green leaf has absorbed all color rays except green. The rays we name green are reflected back. We specify an object by the one quality it has rejected and hurled in our faces.

If I was sure of anything this morning, it was the blue of my turtleneck. Even if its particular blueness was perceived only through my eyes, it was still blue. And it was true. But now I am wearing a not-blue turtleneck. Wearing it to complement my not-blue eyes. My eyes that have been looking for a god in an unblue sky.

In the search for truth I am dazzled by rejected rays of light. I am confounded by objects that will not reveal their essence. By what appears but is not. With all I know, with language, art, and science, I still stand naked with Eve in the garden, tempted and betrayed at every blink of my eyes by apples that are every color but red.

Joyce Thompson

JOYCE THOMPSON
Novelist, short-story writer, writing instructor

Interview

by Linda Davies

Joyce Thompson is the author of six novels: The Blue Chair, Hothouse, Merry-Go-Round, Conscience Place, Bones, *and the soon-to-be-released* Paradise Illustrated. *She has also written two collections of short fiction:* 35-Cent Thrills *and* East Is West of Here. *Joyce teaches fiction workshops at universities and writing conferences throughout the West. She had just completed three weeks of teaching when she made time to meet with me at Cannon Beach on the Oregon coast.*

Joyce Thompson

DAVIES: *This is your sixth novel you're just finishing now,* Paradise Illustrated. *Is it something that you want to talk about? Have you gotten any response yet to the work?*

THOMPSON: Well, it's a dark comic novel that aspires to a kind of tenderness. I got a chance to field-test it at the Port Townsend

Writers' Conference at Centrum. Each instructor does a craft lecture and a reading; I read the first four chapters, which had not been seen by human eye or heard by human ear.

I like to read to a dark house. You don't see the audience, but you feel it much more acutely. And, of course, you hear it. And I got everything back from that audience I might have hoped for—there were just huge walls of laughter rising up, and then, when the mood turned, pin-drop silence. It was one of the great nights of my life, actually. The response was warm and open and generous and vocal. It felt very good. But the whole book has felt good.

You have mentioned that doing Bones *[her previous novel] was hard, but healing, for you. I would imagine that, at the end of any major work, you get some kind of gift from it?*

Oh, I think the gift has been very delayed with *Bones*, and I don't know what it is. I think I'm still waiting for the gift, although there is a certain relief in that I don't have to tell those stories anymore. I unloaded a great deal of psychic baggage, in a way that's almost embarrassing but maybe, I think, maybe useful. I think it transcends therapy. I certainly hope so.

Bones is a very dark book and I've had a fair amount of shame and difficulty about it, largely because some events in my life coincided so eerily with the fiction. I think you're vulnerable to superstition about those kinds of coincidences when you're in the space from which you create your fictions.

Do you think that's superstition?

The rationalist in me says, of course it's coincidence, but it's happened enough in the course of fifteen years of writing novels that the more open, vulnerable, perhaps mystical person doesn't believe it could possibly be entirely coincidence. And yet it's such arrogance to think that you have hauled something into being in the material world out of your own imagination. It may just be a case of simply bumping up against a piece of reality that we've never bumped into before. I don't know how it happens, but there is often an amazing coincidence between fiction and life. Certainly in my characters. It sounds foolish to say it, yet when you experience it, you tend to take it rather seriously.

In several of your stories I notice an absence of safety—fear, terror even— that comes in occasionally. You create it, portray it so realistically that I'm inclined to think that you know those things. I remember in a particular story, the line "If my father is strong, am I safe?"

I've been thinking about that a lot lately. Actually, in the story, it goes through a progression. It starts out with the premise, If my father is strong, I am safe. Then, If my father is not strong, am I safe? If *I* am strong, am I safe? Am I strong? I suspect possibly that the process of liberation, a kind of ritual liberation, is something every child has to go through, but it may be particularly important to the female child to work through these steps.

I was just thinking that I'm one of those weird people who is rarely afraid on a dark street or in a bad neighborhood, but my sense, I think, has always been of home as the dangerous place. The intimate setting is the most dangerous. The place in which we are anonymous, we are much safer. I think the notion of home feeling like a haven is learned. But I do think we all know these fears. It's a basic part of being human. How do you make the planet seem a hospitable place? We all have to domesticate it one way or another.

I love the photo you sent of yourself for the author profile page in our first issue—the little girl looking at the giant, somewhat menacing shadow of a very big person. And she's laughing. It seemed to me to reflect some basic courage, bravery.

The kid *[Joyce, at about age four]* has the right idea because she *is* laughing at it, and I think that's a very valid and powerful way to domesticate the shadow. Though we end up laughing at inappropriate things sometimes. I know my new book will offend some people by virtue of the things it laughs at. Death, sex—you know, the big issues. It begins with the line "Henry died the way he always wanted to. He was fifty-nine years old and having an orgasm." I mean, where do you go from there? If you're into piety—

You're not going to like it.

Right. There's something else about that picture, too. I didn't notice it at first, but that little girl has a rumpled little shadow of her own. She can't see it, because it's behind her, but there it is, a darkness of her very own. Nobody is exempt.

What basic things drive you, Joyce? What things are essential to your being?

Essential to my being would be the opportunity to live creatively and to, in some at least modest way, make art—to be able to not leave my circumstances unchanged but to be able, I guess, to take a creator's license and responsibility in dealing with the world. That's very important. Good friends are extremely important; my children are extremely important; exercise, sport, being outdoors are important. Water and mountains and weather and light. Love is extremely important. Actually, operating as much as possible out of love, as a writer, as a teacher, as a parent, as a friend, is essential to me. As kind of the basic premise.

When you write, what is it you strive to create?

Well, I have enormous respect for the power and flexibility of language. I don't believe that there's one set of words in proper order that will do the job. It fascinates me, how simply shifting the same grammatical and syntactical elements within one sentence can change the whole universe. You can reverse cause and effect simply by moving words around; you can make different things the agent of whatever happens; you can bring some things into the foreground and diminish others just simply within the boundaries of one sentence. There's a delight in playing with the language at that level.

I think you're always searching through the language to reality beyond it. The language is often smarter than I am, than the writer is. I often feel like an idiot savant when I'm writing. It's a very intuitive process. There is a certain abrogation of ego, and it happens through the agent of language. It's difficult to explain that and I'm not sure it's the same for all writers. I know some people feel that composition is a real act of arrogance, an assertion of the ego, but I find that when the writing is going its best, it's a real absorption of the ego in the task, a laying aside of it. It's a pretty direct exchange between the language and whatever envisioned reality there is. I think that's one reason that I like doing it so much. I don't get in my own way nearly as much when I write as I do in some of the other things I do in life. There's something beyond individual self and I think, to an extent, I write to experience that.

I think that many creative people, by their creating, manage to do exactly that.

And there's a way in which you can use your own personal history and those of everybody else you may have encountered in your lifetime in a very impersonal way.

Which is very freeing.

It is. Sex is good for that. Those are the two major activities in my life in which I can escape my own consciousness and my own little tiny ego-centered self. So I find both activities very precious. I prize those things in this life that I don't stop doing to answer the telephone.

Joyce, if a person who knew you fairly well were going to try to succinctly describe you to another person, what would they say?

I'm going to sidestep this a little bit. I was talking recently with a friend of a similar age about the necessity to claim who we are and what we know. It's so difficult for some of us. It's much easier to move through the world feeling fat and ugly, or small and weak, or ineffectual, or trivial and ignorant, or whatever those disclaimers are, in the face of enormous evidence to the contrary. If you're lucky, you simply have good friends who get real tired of hearing it and say bullshit, bullshit, bullshit, every time you begin.

Actually, I think the best response to that is to attempt to be egoless. So that you don't really care that much. You have a sense of taking up space in the world, of moving through it with a certain amount of effectiveness, bumping up against other people and making some impact and yet not being tremendously self-conscious about what adjectives would be used to describe you. I *would* like to be thought of as being benign.

A friend of mine, poet Chris Howell, said, just in the last week, he said, "And one day you wake up and realize that there is in you an absolutely magnificent, vital human being who doesn't even need a name." That's the person I hope I am more and more becoming. You know, you certainly don't need adjectives if you don't need a name.

I understand from some of your students that you're really a superb teacher. What or how should a person write to produce their best work? What do you try to teach your students?

I've just come off a few weeks of very good teaching, and teaching is something I've done a lot of in the last ten years, not as a chosen occupation, but as one that has kind of claimed me as an auxiliary to the business of writing. Partly out of economic necessity. If somebody offers you employment, you tend to say sure, but also out of the opportunity to share. I believe there's almost a sacred responsibility to do that. People have helped me at times when I needed it and you pass on where you can. There's a tremendous joy in working with writers and I've been perhaps rarely blessed with awfully good students over the years, people who are now very well published and have contributed some very fine fictions to the world. I love working with people who are right at the edge of making a serious commitment to their writing. I also love enfranchising the creativity of just about anybody, finding the storyteller in any person who happens by, because there really is one.

This sounds like that love thing you were talking about.

It very much is. It's a very exciting thing to do and I think over ten years there's been a process of shifting ego balance. I am so delighted with the two conferences I've just taught because, somehow, in a funny way, I spent less of myself, of my own personal inner stuff. I haven't felt like I was having to hold the plane in the sky by myself. None of this white goddess shit, and yet, in some way, I've given more because my ego hasn't been involved in the transaction. I feel far less drained.

I think people often come to a writing class, or to a writing teacher, at the point where they need some key permission, and for years I accepted that role as a permission giver. I think it's wrong to create that kind of dependence. I mean, it works to an extent, but I think the better teacher manages to somehow enable the student to give him- or herself permission. It's a totally different kind of transaction. It's much more powerful. And the gift to the student is a gift of him- or herself rather than the teacher self. But that's something that takes a long time to even understand. I'm sure I've passed out a whole lot of permissions in my time that have done the job anyhow because people were ready for them and knew how to use them and it didn't much matter that I was being grandiose issuing them.

What kind of permission do people look for?

It varies a lot. Often people simply want permission to take what they perceive as a risk. It may be to deal with certain materials that feel very risky or threatening. It may be to make a serious reorganization of one's life in order to make writing a primary value, to try to live by it. That's a very major decision which nobody can make for you. The only thing a teacher can say is, you're good enough that if you gave it your best shot the work produced would certainly be worth it. If you want to live that way is another question. That's the best you can ever tell someone.

I had an older man student at Centrum who was a very accomplished writer who's published at least as many novels as I have. They're detective novels, kind of an adventure genre.

The man is tremendously bright, very sophisticated, and wants to write a much more complex, thoroughgoing fiction. He wants to be sort of a gentler, more grown-up, intellectual writer and he wanted someone to tell him that was okay. He's dying in that tight rubber suit and wants to break out of it and it's the time to come for courage and have someone say, "Yeah, you're good enough to do that, you have a perfect right to do that." Ultimately, he has to give himself permission.

It's really funny how we invest so much power in people outside ourselves, when what we really need is some sense of our own power. It's a game we play. It really is. It's built into the culture in all our rituals and I'm not sure it's wrong, but it's only a ritual because ultimately what you do need to do is to claim your own power and make your own decisions.

I think I'm just beginning to lock into a better way of teaching that I find really exciting. The energy moves in a different way, in a much more healthy way, I think.

I never cease to be amazed how much people do when offered a nurturing environment and a lot of challenge. I try to be both very nurturing and extremely demanding as I teach. I don't think there's a great service in not showing people what the challenges are, even imagining them much better, better than they are, because then they go out and do it. I am constantly surprised by how far people can come, how fast, given some tiny shift in the internal landscape that lets them feel what they can do if they truly want to.

There's a wonderful book by Italo Calvino, the recently deceased Italian novelist and critic, which comes down to an image of one four-hundred-year-old man in the heart of the Brazilian rain forest who is the source of all stories. And I think that's an incredibly potent image because it means we can commit ourselves to stories and not be so concerned about authorship. I think that's a good way to feel when you're teaching. It's a good way to feel when your colleague writes something that just blows you away and you're tempted to be envious of someone else's work.

But, I've almost come to believe, as a teacher, that stories do have a life of their own. There's something that happens when I approach somebody else's story in process—and I think calling something "in process" is permission to approach it not as an artifact, but as a living thing. A story can tell you a lot about what it wants to be if you listen to the story. I think if there is a real strength in my teaching, it may be having learned to listen to stories very attentively. And that kind of transcends simple skills with language or editing or, you know, a mastery of certain concepts. It has to do with really treating a story as a psychic entity that does have a certain personality, that has a certain will, that has a certain intention, and it can be very revealing, while it's still in process, of the person who is creating it.

That's a very appealing idea.

Well, I could attribute this all to my razor-sharp mind, but I think I'd probably be lying. It *is* fairly intuitive. It's a place where mind and intuition meet and abet each other. You know, when you get them together you can really hear a lot of what a story says. Another important thing in teaching is simply giving students or fellow writers or less experienced writers the sense of possibility—that there are many ways to do things. And this is certainly a gift I will accept myself in some circumstances because we do tend to get very focused and hidebound and see fewer possibilities than actually exist. There are many paths to follow, many possible ways for characters to go or stories to turn. Really to kind of blast open the creative consciousness to different kinds of possibilities is often a gift that a teacher can give. And can receive, that any writer can receive, because we can get awfully left-brain sometimes.

Who has given you permission?

When I was about fifteen, my teacher, Joe Medlicott, gave me permission to want and to try to be a writer. When I was about twenty-five, Rosellen Brown, a writer I very much admire, told me I was the real thing—a writer. She sort of discovered me.

A few years ago, I went to Florida, to the Atlantic Center for the Arts, where they have a program where artists at mid-career get to spend time with established masters in their respective fields. I expected to be matching wits with Stanley Elkin, but he became ill and couldn't come. Doris Grumbach was there instead.

Now there is a woman with *standards*. She is both very bracing and very generous. I suppose what she gave me was permission to stop asking for permission. You *are* a writer, woman. Of course, it's not easy; it probably won't be lucrative; and it's quite possible nobody will appreciate your work until you're dead—that, only if you're lucky—but it's who you are and what you have to do. So get on with it. Doris gave me permission to keep on keepin' on. As she has done.

If you're very impressed by someone's work, why is that?

Well, because I've been moved, because I've been rearranged, because I've been entertained. There are a million answers to that. Because, with an alphabet of twenty-six letters, someone has taken me to a new place, stopped my world for a moment, rearranged it, burned their characters, their imaginations, and illusions into my neural pathways, probably for all time, made the rhythms of my heart and body sync up to the rhythms of their language, invaded my dreams. I think one of the ways that you recognize wonderful work is that it incites in you the impulse to say thank you.

I really appreciate people who can keep me up all night. And I'm not talking about what you think I am, although that's not bad either, but, boy, if you can just do it with words, that's good, when you don't feel that you're in bed alone.

You are one of those rare writers who manages to put food on the table, if not necessarily dessert, with your work, and your stories are very down to earth, real world sort of stories. You've obviously got an awareness of how to take care of your children, how to take care of yourself, how to live with your feet on the ground and how to get out there and get things done. Now, on the other hand, I understand that you do tarot cards and clearly you're interested in spiritual, mystical things. How did that come about and how does that affect your life?

First of all, I would agree with Mark Twain that there is a god- or goddess-shaped hole in the center of every human being that needs to be filled with *something*. We all walk around with that. Some of us are more aware of it than others, and our growing-up environment offers things that may or may not fit that hole for any individual one of us. I think writing may be what incited the reverence and provided the practice that's introduced me to a more spiritual dimension, coming out of a pretty rational and agnostic, if not atheistic, family background. Although I was fascinated to hear someone in the family describe my grandparents as "socialists with a Ouija board." Maybe it's simply in the genes.

I remember the first time language kicked in for me. I was the same age my son is now. I told stories and loved stories and was a reader before that, but I got rolling on a poem—I'm sure it was very stupid—but then language passed through me, and I could do things with it—or maybe *it* could do things with *me*—that made me new and different, and whatever dance was going on between us felt like nothing I'd ever felt before. Language does call some people in that way.

I think we approach our work as writers for different reasons. Some people are called by the language, and then they have to learn to see the stories and find out what they mean and all those other things. Some people are called by story and then have to learn to love and use the language. When it's language that calls, it tends to be an early call. This is a gross generalization, but I think that people who are called earlier are called by language; people who are called later are usually called because of the stories they have to tell.

Anyway, I experienced a profound sense of there being something outside myself, beyond myself, that I wanted to be able to serve and to experience for a whole lifetime. That something is powerful enough to cause me to fairly continuously try to reinvent myself and my commitment, so it *will* last a lifetime. So, maybe my sense of mysticism comes almost empirically out of the experience of being a writer.

You are stepping out into woo-woo-land when you undertake both the total arrogance and the total humility required to attempt to conjure new worlds and convincing human beings out of black squiggles on a piece of paper. You know there's some agency of magic that transcends reason right there. And it means that, on a daily basis, you're seeking to open parts of your consciousness that aren't necessarily accessed by rational living. There's a lot of power in those places, and the more you visit them, the more you credit their existence and you credit their power, I think.

In terms of tarot cards and astrology and other things, I find them interesting primarily as very ancient metaphoric systems that were brought into creation because people needed a way to talk about certain things. There are a lot of different diagnostic and divinatory systems that have arisen probably out of every human culture that the planet has ever spawned. We make stories, we make metaphors, in order to be able to talk about things that we perceive to be true of human experience in some sort of organized fashion. I don't give total adherence to any system, but there's a lot of wisdom encoded in them, if only because they give a way to talk about things that might otherwise be real difficult to domesticate into our consciousness. Am I a literal believer in any? No, but am I a believer in the freeing power of metaphor to increase our insight into ourselves and our fellow human beings? Absolutely.

Thank you, Joyce. It's been a pleasure.

Susan Burmeister (signature)

SUSAN BURMEISTER
Man across the Aisle

Bruce had noticed the way his wife's pink sweater made her cheeks rosy and her mouth positively bloom, and so he decided against telling her that the tag on her sweater was flipped up, not counting on the solicitude of the man across the aisle on the train who simply reached over and tucked it in for her. His fingers rested only a moment on the back of her neck, the sheerest moment, but Bruce felt his wife shiver at the touch. The stranger felt it, too, and smiled.

Bruce's wife responded to the stranger's smile by putting her left hand on her husband's leg.

The beverage cart wheeled up and the stranger requested a small bottle of red, two glasses, and then leaned across the aisle to ask Bruce if he would like to join them in some Bordeaux. Bruce declined, looking at his watch to show his disfavor. It was not even two o'clock in the afternoon. The vendor uncorked the bottle, had the stranger nod his approval, and poured two full plastic cups, placing them both along with the rest of the bottle onto the table in front of the stranger. The stranger handed him a £10 note, received a £1 in change, and then gave one crimson cup to Bruce's wife.

"A toast," he said simply, "to you."

Glimmer Train Stories, Issue 5, Winter 1993
©1991 Susan Burmeister

Bruce's wife held the cup in both hands and appeared not to know how to respond. "Well, thank you," she said at last, and they tapped plastic rims.

The bottle was finished after two hours of talk and shortly before their arrival in Glasgow. Bruce's wife asked the stranger if she could keep the empty bottle. "The label is very attractive," she explained to Bruce while the stranger located the cork for her.

Bruce and his wife got off the train. The stranger remained. Bruce felt his wife lagging behind as they left the platform and turned around just in time to see her accept the stranger's blown kiss through the window.

The incident was not mentioned that evening other than in passing, when Bruce suggested she might wish to forgo wine with dinner. She agreed, but then asked the waiter to please bring her a gin and tonic with lemon.

Bruce was quiet during the meal and later when they unpacked in their hotel room. His wife was quiet, too. "Tired," he said, but not so tired that he couldn't make love to her when she finished her bath, and again early the next morning just after sunrise. She drifted back to sleep, but Bruce flipped off their travel alarm that was set for seven-thirty a.m. and remained awake.

Finally at eight o'clock he slipped out of bed, washed and dressed, and packed for both of them, letting his wife sleep until just ten minutes before they had to leave for the station. He answered her horror when she saw the clock register ten minutes until nine by explaining that he knew she could well use the extra sleep after their long journey the day before, and besides, he'd already packed them both up. Bruce called for a taxi and then sat on the edge of the bed watching her comb her hair and scramble into the clothes he'd kept out for her.

When she reached for her cosmetic bag, he stood up and announced that it was time to leave, the taxi had arrived. "No need for makeup, dear. It's just the train again today," and took the bags to the taxi outside, thinking of the pink sweater he'd left behind on the back of the bathroom door.

Settled into their seats on the train to Liverpool, Bruce ordered a glass of orange juice, and he spilled a little onto the front of her white blouse as he took it from the vendor. He sat back in his seat, sipping his juice, satisfied with the empty seats across the aisle, and watched Scotland pass by outside his window until he slid into a light doze.

He did not see his wife take out her cosmetic bag and apply her lipstick. He did not see the next stranger get on two stops later and take the seat across the aisle. And he did not notice the bee resting on his wife's right shoulder, until the hand reached across the aisle to brush it away.

$\mathscr{S}$TORIES GONE BY

Past issues are available for $9 each.

B. MULLIGAN
1991

Take a look at this lineup!

Because we can hear the strike of her shoes on the basement stairs, and the click of the lock as she turns it, everyone is looking at the beige door when Emmaline steps through it.

from "Who Lives in the Basement" by Joyce Thompson

He'd been steaming ever since he read it, stomped around the house, threw the section with the article in it to the floor, snapped at his kids when they came downstairs for breakfast, snapped at his wife before he left the house.

from "Hand" by Stephen Dixon

It took all night for Uncle Zack to thaw, and we hardly got a word out of him. He managed the tea all right and a steaming bowl of chicken broth. It was good to get rid of that broth, I tell you; the can had haunted our cupboard for months.

from "And the Greatest of These" by Louis Gallo

Alfredo has a desperate mental picture of himself as the sole point of resistance, like a crumbling wall that stands between a coastal village and a violent sea. Fear hangs in the air; it clings to his shirt and coats his hands.

from "The Net" by Peter Gordon

160